Praise for Cindy Procter-King

"Cindy Procter-King is a master storyteller. Not only do her characters invite the readers into the drama, the humor is non-stop. Comedy is a hard genre to write but Cindy Procter-King does it easily."

— The Road to Romance on HEAD OVER HEELS

"What a set-up for a comedy of errors! Everything that can go wrong in this scenario does go wrong, and the reader is well entertained by the comedic chaos."

— Fallen Angel Reviews on HEAD OVER HEELS

"I really enjoyed *Borrowing Alex*. It was smart and funny without being overdone. The characters do some pretty funny things in the name of love. I am definitely looking forward to reading the next book I find by Cindy Procter-King."

— Joyfully Reviewed on BORROWING ALEX

"I really like romantic comedy as a genre, but it takes some really good writing to make me laugh. This book made me laugh."

— Fallen Angel Reviews on BORROWING ALEX

"'*Getting Over Brett*' is everything a romantic comedy should be!...a very funny, light and easy romance that will leave a big goofy smile on your face!"

— InD'tale Magazine on GETTING OVER BRETT

"*Getting Over Brett* is a top-of-the-line read. It has everything you could possibly want in a modern romance. It's fun and playful at times, full of flirty banter, then deeply romantic and emotional at its heart. Somehow, it's both sweet and sexy all at the same time!"

— Julianne MacLean, USA Today Bestselling Author

"Cindy Procter-King presents readers with a suspenseful snapshot of a romantic comedy... loaded with humor, this is a must-read."

— Night Owl Reviews on PICTURE IMPERFECT

"Procter-King has written a 'home' for all of us. Destiny Falls is the place that holds your first love, your first triumph..."

— RT Book Reviews on WHERE SHE BELONGS

Before Brady

Also by Cindy Procter-King

Steamy RomCom

Love & Other Calamities

RomCom Series

Deceiving Derek (Book 1)

Catching Claire (Book 2)

Just Janie (Book 4)

Trusting Trey (Book 5)

Love in the Pacific Northwest

Stand-alone Romantic Comedy

Head Over Heels (Book 1)

Borrowing Alex (Book 2)

Getting Over Brett (Book 3)

Contemporary Romance

Single Title Romance

Picture Imperfect (Sassy Mystery Romance)

Where She Belongs (Emotional Small Town Romance)

Before Brady

CINDY PROCTER-KING

BEFORE BRADY

Copyright © 2023 Cindy Procter-King

All rights reserved.

No part of this publication maybe be reproduced in any form or by any electronic or mechanical means, including information storage and retrieval systems, or otherwise, without explicit written permission from the author, except in the case of brief quotations used in book reviews and articles.

This is a work of fiction. Characters, names, places, events, incidents, scenarios, opinions, brands, media, are of the author's imagination or are used fictitiously. Any resemblance to actual incidents, locales, or persons, living or dead, is entirely coincidental.

Before Brady © 2023 by Cindy Procter-King

Published by Blue Orchard Books

Cover by The Killion Group

ISBN: 978-0-9880884-8-1 (eBook)

ISBN: 978-1-989113-08-0 (Print)

For my dad, who loves with his whole heart

Chapter One

Saturday night, July 15th
Countdown to Tania and Trey's wedding: 14 days
(unless...)

"READY?" Alicia Maxwell asked her assistant, Lettie. They stood in the reception hall kitchen, wearing matching gold T-shirts and mint-green miniskirts. On the other side of the swinging door, three hundred thirtieth anniversary party guests laughed and clapped as the host delivered a heartfelt toast to his wife.

Lettie's brown eyes widened. "Y-yes." The hesitation in the younger woman's voice suggested otherwise.

Alicia touched her assistant's arm. "Promise you're not just saying that? Because I can do it." Although she didn't want to, if it could be helped. Alicia didn't want Brady Jacobs to catch sight of her at all during his parents' celebration. Which meant staying in the catering kitchen while Lettie carried in the slicing cake for three large cupcake towers sitting on the dessert table.

Lettie drew in a ragged breath. "I'll make last night up to you if it's the last thing I do."

Alicia smiled. "I wouldn't want it to be the *last* thing you do. Please don't worry about the first batch of cupcakes. I need you, Lettie. We're a team."

Lettie shook her head. Her springy curls bounced. "You're my boss. And I'm a nitwit."

"That's not true." Given the twenty-two-year-old's baking experience and delicious sample cupcakes, Lettie required more supervision than Alicia had expected. Nothing more. "We're both bagged." Flat-out exhausted.

Lettie's lower lip trembled. "Because of me."

"No. Because of *my* choices." Alicia inhaled, her frustration directed at herself. In her quest to grow Bitty Cakes as quickly as possible, she'd accepted too many catering jobs this summer. Squeezing in the Jacobs anniversary had increased a heavy workload. The stress was doing a number on herself as well as her employees. If Alicia were into assigning blame, *she* was the nitwit.

Last night, she'd jumped at Lettie's offer to bake three hundred cupcakes on her own. In hindsight, not a smart move, but Alicia understood Lettie's need to prove herself. As the baby of the Maxwell family and the only girl out of five kids, Alicia had struggled not to feel singled out, while also somehow getting lost in the mix, since the early death of her mom.

Before abandoning Lettie yesterday to handle the humongous anniversary order, Alicia had described tweaks to the shop's popular mint chocolate chip recipe. Unfortunately, she'd neglected to highlight an important ingredient adjustment.

Um, yeah. Not so bright.

Believing everything under control, Alicia hurried home to host a friend's combination bridal shower and bachelorette party. Lettie was to text or call with questions. Alicia hadn't heard a word.

She *should* have followed up with her assistant. If the shower hadn't escalated into a rowdy extravaganza, she would have checked in with Lettie earlier.

As it was, the muscular stripper whipped the women into a frenzy. The winner of the scavenger hunt became enamored with another guest's brother. The bride took 'tipsy' to a new level, which remained a bit of a mystery because Alicia hadn't noticed Tania tossing them back.

As the festivities wound down, Alicia walked the bride to a nearby park before driving her home. Everything had felt relatively manageable to that point.

Way too long later, she'd spotted her phone dead in her purse. Upon plugging in, several panicked texts and voicemails flooded her screen. Each from an overwhelmed Lettie, requesting Alicia's help and guidance.

Alicia had needed to redo three...hundred... cupcakes...while her assistant slept off a well-deserved rest.

She stifled a yawn. "Let's put last night behind us," she urged Lettie. "How about we channel serenity?" She swept up her hands in a reassuring gesture. "We're calm. We're collected. We take charge of our actions and our lives."

Lettie repeated the motions. "We're calm. We're collected. *Phew*. Thank you, Alicia."

"You're welcome." Alicia stepped to the kitchen's swinging door and cracked it open. She peered inside the hall.

Twenty feet away, Brady's mom joined his dad at the decorated podium. The couple addressed the crowd, and a spike of unease skittered up Alicia's spine. A natural response, she told herself. At this early phase of her business, coordinating desserts for large occasions required every ounce of her focus. Tonight was no different.

Except...except...tonight *was* different, damn it. Alicia chewed her lip. Although she hadn't spotted him, knowing Brady Jacobs sat at a family table sent pinpricks of sensation along her limbs and across her face.

She couldn't allow anything else to go wrong at *his* parents' shindig. She hadn't fully recovered from their last encounter. Obsessing over his unsettling effect on her nervous system took a toll she lacked the time or energy to process.

She focused her attention onto his mom, Maureen. One word from the woman would signal the delivery of the slicing cake.

"Dessert!" Maureen announced, and cheers filled the enormous room.

Alicia glanced around the hall. The family and friends in attendance spanned generations from a crying baby to a ninety-year-old man. Children played between the crowded tables. Teenagers huddled along a wall. An exasperated-looking woman raced after a toddler clutching a cupcake. The adorable monster squealed with glee each time he evaded the harried woman's grasp.

Despite the commotion, Don and Maureen Jacobs exchanged loving smiles. The couple planned to feed each other bites of cake, like a bride and groom. Alicia sighed. They were so sweet.

She looked back at Lettie, who picked up the six-inch slicing cake on a sturdy tray.

"Piece o' cake," Lettie said with a grin.

"That's the spirit." Alicia opened the kitchen door, and Lettie walked out.

A boisterous, "Hurrah!" boomed from the crowd.

Alicia peeked into the hall again, monitoring Lettie's progress toward the dessert table, situated to the left of Brady's parents. After accounting for the cupcake theft, two-hundred-ninety-nine tasty desserts adorned the display towers. The edible gold stars Brady's mom had requested decorated the mint-green frosting spirals. The spangles reminded Alicia of Brady's police badge. Although his star was silver. And bigger. A *lot* bigger.

Oh, for—

She shook her head. The size of Brady's badge wasn't relevant. Tonight's cupcakes looked and tasted divine. She had consumed several lopsided extras to make sure.

Her gaze found him—although she hadn't been looking for the guy. He sat at a round table near the podium, a frown creasing his handsome face. Alicia took in his short-trimmed chestnut-brown hair with a hint of curl at the crown. Her heart did an annoying leap-for-joy thing. *Down, girl.*

She allowed herself a scan of his broad chest in a white dress shirt before hauling her gaze back up to his expression. Her eyebrows arched. Why was he frowning? Was he surprised *she* wasn't bringing in the slicing cake? Was he wondering why she hadn't shown her face tonight?

Not that it mattered, but let him stew over—uh, consider the ramifications of issuing her a speeding ticket three weeks ago. Yeah, let him.

The moment she'd recognized him at her car window, she'd insisted he not treat her differently from any other driver, even if she was his commander's daughter. It was embarrassing enough that she hadn't realized she was traveling well over the posted limit, so intent had she been on locating the supply store his mom had specified for purchasing the edible stars.

True, Alicia had made a valuable new contact in the bakery industry, but the fact remained that *Officer* Brady Jacobs had caught her with her pedal to the infernal metal. In her family, traffic infractions were grounds for lecturing to the extreme.

"Just doing my job," Brady had said that fateful Saturday. He'd tipped his police hat, his mesmerizing green eyes twinkling.

The memory swirled, and Alicia's body warmed.

As he'd returned to his patrol unit, she'd eyed his butt in her side mirror. Again, only later had she noticed a lower speed recorded on her ticket, saving her a hefty fine and eliminating a hike in her insurance rates.

Brady had orchestrated the favor behind her back! The man had some nerve.

Squaring her shoulders, Alicia scoped out Lettie's snail-like progress toward the dessert table. Maureen smiled and stepped closer to the girl.

Brady sprang off his chair.

Alicia followed his gaze to a glob of frosting on the floor.

In Lettie's path.

"Oh, no," she whispered, extending a hand, heart ticking like a doomsday countdown. "L-Lettie," she said louder. "Watch your step."

Lettie skidded on the frosting and crashed to her backside.

The cake catapulted into the air.

A collective gasp burst from the crowd.

Alicia dashed into the hall. *"Oh, my God,"* she muttered hoarsely. "This cannot be happening."

But it was.

Brady's mom leaped toward the cake. Maureen's arms scooped forward as if she were trying to catch a football. Or a bridal bouquet.

"Look out," Don shouted.

A young woman rushed over. "Mom. No!"

Brady tried holding back his mom, but Maureen flung off his arm.

The cake hit Maureen's ivory lace dress. Mint-green frosting smashed into her cleavage. Chunks of cake spewed into the air and onto the ground. The tray clattered to the floor.

Maureen swiped at her bodice. "Our cake! Don, I thought I had it in my sights."

Alicia reached the family. "Maureen! I'm so sorry."

"We're good," Don responded, not unkindly. He nodded toward Lettie, who wept on the ground, cradling her head. "See to your assistant."

"Of course." Alicia kneeled beside her employee. "Here, Lettie. Take my hand."

Lettie groaned, sobs wracking her shoulders.

Alicia alternated between scanning her assistant for injuries and gawking as Brady grabbed two fistfuls of paper napkins and passed them to his father.

The young woman who'd hurried to Maureen retrieved the tray and disappeared from view. Don wiped his wife's dress as dozens of friends and family gathered close.

A man hoisted a champagne glass. "As Jacobs parties go, this one takes the cupcake!"

The crowd laughed.

Maureen flicked a hand. "I'm all right. It's only cake."

Don dipped a finger into her cleavage and made a show of licking off the frosting. "Tastes great," he declared, digging in for seconds.

The crowd hooted and cheered.

"Don," Maureen cooed. She smiled at Alicia. "Don't worry, honey. Tend to your friend."

Alicia *would* worry. Maureen's dress was a mess, and hundreds of guests had witnessed a cupcake disaster of epic proportions. Phone cameras abounded. Bitty Cakes would become a laughing-stock. And poor Lettie—

Brady lowered beside Alicia and her employee. "Stay back, everyone," he said, holding up a hand. His gaze flicked to Lettie's. "Don't move."

Alicia waved him away. "I have First Aid."

"I can handle this."

"So can I." She stared into his dazzling moss-green eyes. She refused to allow them to hypnotize her into compliance. Lettie was her responsibility.

Lettie wailed. "I'm a failure!"

Alicia examined her assistant's head and body. "Lettie, shh. Where does it hurt?"

Lettie sniffled. "I didn't hit my head. I thought I did, but my butt is sore."

Brady nodded. "I'll take you to the hospital."

Alicia lifted her chin. "I'll take her."

His gaze swept over the crowded room. "You have your hands full," he pointed out.

"Right." With Lettie out of commission, Alicia represented the sole member of the dessert catering staff. Thankfully, a second slicing cake sat in the kitchen. Call her paranoid, but after her mistake with the recipe, she'd considered it prudent to bake a spare.

A dark-skinned guy around Lettie's age crouched beside them. "I'm more than happy to drive Lettie to the hospital. We've met before. Haven't we, Lets?" The fellow patted Lettie's arm.

Lettie's eyes opened from between splayed fingers. "Y-yes." She gave the dude a watery smile. "Thank you."

Brady nodded at the younger man. "Way to step up, Nelson." He glanced at Alicia. "Our parents live on the same road. I've known Nelson since he was in diapers."

"TMI," Nelson quipped, helping Lettie.

The younger woman winced as she stood. "I'm sorry, Alicia. I shouldn't have taken this job. I don't have the experience."

Alicia popped to her feet. "That's okay. Um, what do you mean?"

"My mom—" Lettie sucked in a breath. "My mom baked my sample cupcakes."

"What?" Alicia's pulse blipped. During Lettie's five months of employment, Alicia had supervised the girl through countless recipes. "I checked your references. The bakery in Auburn gave a glowing review."

"That was a friend. Working at a cupcake shop sounded fun. My friend said I would learn. But this job is stressful. I can't take it anymore. I quit."

Alicia's jaw hit the floor. Lettie had chosen *now* to come clean? In front of hundreds of potential customers?

Brady leaned close. "Let's go to the kitchen," he murmured. "I'll help."

"I can manage on my own," Alicia muttered, cursing the ticklish sensation rippling up her neck.

His mom stepped forward. "Alicia, please accept my apologies. I pressured you into taking this job on short notice. Brady said his fellow officers gobble your cupcakes every chance they get. And your father—well, Brady says the man just raves."

Alicia's cheeks burned. She didn't want to hear about Brady's connection to her dad. She loved her family, but she'd worked hard to achieve her independence.

"I will take care of everything tonight," she reiterated with a stiff smile. She glimpsed Nelson and Lettie exiting the building. She returned her attention to Brady's mom. "Maureen, I'll pay for your dry cleaning and discount the catering bill." She backed toward the kitchen. "I'll get the spare slicing cake—"

"Don't worry your sweet head about it." Maureen paused. "Oh. Did you say you have a spare?"

Alicia nodded. Her one saving grace today. She had a spare.

"I'll be back soon," she said, arrowing for the kitchen. Oh, boy, she would never hear the end about tonight. Once her dad and her four older brothers caught wind of this latest upheaval, they would fall all over her with advice and good intentions instead of allowing her to stand—or fail, if it came to that—on her own.

"Alicia, wait." Brady's deep voice resonated with concern and earthy sexiness.

But she dared not glance back. She dared not allow the man to slip beneath her defenses for one enticing moment. He touched an emotion deep inside her which could swallow her up in romantic fantasies.

She couldn't allow that. *Could not*. She needed to stay on point. In her life and in her business.

He needed to find another woman to rescue.

Chapter Two

Hands on hips, Brady tracked Alicia Maxwell's brisk return to the kitchen. Her sleek dark hair swung around her shoulders. Her short skirt swayed. Her long legs chewed up the distance. Hadn't she heard him call out for her to wait? Or was she avoiding him?

His mom pumped a fist. "Look at that initiative," Mom gushed, nudging Dad. "Nothing stops that girl. Don, she had the foresight to bake a spare slicing cake. I'm impressed."

Alicia reached the swinging door and punched it open. Then she was gone.

Brady returned the few steps to his parents. His younger sister, Kristi, now at the dessert table after clearing away the cake tray, rearranged desserts knocked askew from a child's earlier grab-and-run. Family and friends crowded his parents, several wielding phones while others cleaned crumbs off the floor.

"You're right," Brady said to his mom. "Alicia is tackling the problem at hand." *While* pretending he didn't exist—her standard operating procedure at their every encounter, it seemed. Why? Because her father was his commander? Or had Brady screwed up in a way only obvious to her in the ten months since they'd met?

He should leave the mystery alone, but Alicia Maxwell intrigued him on multiple levels. He itched to figure her out.

"Alicia Maxwell is a force of nature," his mom said, smoothing a hand over his shoulder.

"A lot like my Mo," Dad added, kissing Mom's cheek.

"Oh, Don. Bitty Cakes will take off like a rocket. You two wait and see. Alicia's treats are smack-your-lips delicious."

"I'll vouch for that," Dad said, licking a finger and pressing the tip to the crumbs sprinkled across Mom's upper chest. Dad held his finger toward the crowd before slurping the digit clean.

Their friends and family cheered.

Brady rolled his eyes but couldn't suppress a smile. His parents were beyond special, acting like love-struck college students with each other half the time. Yeah, their behavior was embarrassing. Their banter and affection also comprised a huge part of their charm.

Mom laughed with Dad. Smiling at the multitude of phone cameras, she proclaimed, "Everyone, please enjoy the cupcakes." She gave an exaggerated wink. "The ones on the dessert table."

The guests, deep in celebration mode, swarmed the cupcake towers. Dad signaled the DJ to spin some tunes. As several folks got into the dancing, Brady's sister came toward Mom with a pristine cupcake perched on her outstretched palm.

"Here, Mom," Kristi said. "This beauty will help you forget the slip-and-slide."

Mom accepted the tiny cake. "Thank you, sweetie."

"I ran into Alicia in the kitchen," Kristi went on. "We exchanged numbers. I'll text her when you and Dad are ready for the spare slicing cake."

Mom patted Kristi's cheek. "That's my clever baby." Mom savored a bite of cupcake before breaking off three frosting-slathered chunks. She allotted the first piece to Dad and the others to Kristi and Brady.

Brady popped his morsel into his mouth and chewed. The chocolate-mint flavor of the cake and the silky decadence of the chips melted on his tongue.

"Delicious," he mumbled.

Alicia's treats *were* tasty. What he really wanted from the cupcake cutie, though, was a smile. He hadn't imagined the attraction arcing between them during their conversation at her dad's backyard barbecue last September. He couldn't be that clueless. Her interest had reflected in her pretty blue gaze and in the softness of her voice as they'd talked.

But then he'd crossed an unforeseen and invisible line by asking her out for coffee. She'd made an excuse about not dating cops before developing an intense fascination with collecting compostable plates and forks.

Brady pushed away the memory. "I'll fetch a clean cloth from the kitchen." The sooner his mother tidied her dress, the sooner guests would stop recording Alicia's misfortune.

Dad fished a damp rag from the dessert table. "No need. Your sister grabbed this one while everyone was staring at your mom's—"

"Don't say it," Brady interrupted, shooting his father a steely glance.

Dad chortled. "A bit of the blarney is in me tonight."

Mom's eyebrows wiggled. "A bit of your blarney might be in me tonight."

Brady groaned. "Mom. Now?"

Dad presented the cloth to Mom like an eighteenth-century courtier addressing a queen. Mom accepted the cloth, and she and Kristi wove through the crowd toward the restrooms.

Dad elbowed Brady. "Alicia might need you in the kitchen, my boy."

Brady shook his head. "She has things under control." Soon, she would appear with the spare slicing cake, resolve no doubt shining in her long-lashed eyes.

Dad shrugged. "It can't hurt to check things out." He motioned a thumb toward the closed kitchen door. "You might even learn she's single."

Alicia's relationship status wasn't the issue. "Dad, she and I have been down that road already. Alicia doesn't date cops." Brady had gotten the message loud and clear last fall. A few days following her father's work barbecue, Brady messaged her on social media. Twice. She hadn't responded. Twice.

Getting the hint, he'd screwed his head back on and refocused on his job.

Dad snorted. "What are you talking about? Her father is a cop."

"There are enough of us in her own family, I guess." Alicia's four brothers also worked in law enforcement.

"Bah." Dad pulled a face. "She hasn't met the *right* cop." He lifted his hands. "But who am I to say? Old farts know nothing about romance."

Brady peered toward the shut kitchen door. His dad had read him like a dog-eared book. Absolutely, he wished he and Alicia could get on the right footing. She seemed sweet and kind, and determination radiated off her in waves.

Frankly, he couldn't stop thinking about her. If she weren't special, he would have punted her from his thoughts before Halloween.

Now, the end of July was closing in, and catching her speeding was the highlight of his summer. It appeared Alicia Maxwell was unattainable *and* unforgettable.

He rubbed his chin. Between tonight's dessert accident and the recent traffic stop, had fate handed him an opportunity to find out if her dating restrictions had changed?

Dad, ever the romantic, persisted. "What are you waiting for, son?"

Brady turned toward the kitchen. "Not a damn thing."

Shaking out her hands at her sides, Alicia paced the industrial-style kitchen. "It'll be okay. It'll be okay." She repeated the mantra over and over.

Except how could her life and business ever wind up feeling okay when notifications dinged on her phone every few seconds, announcing another photo or video appearing on social media? Her carefully curated Bitty Cakes profiles were tagged in posts destined to live on forever in the cringeworthy archives of the internet.

She ached to pull herself together and handle this disaster of a night. But, for now, she needed to wait. She needed to place her client's wishes ahead of her own. As much as it killed her to wear a path in the commercial vinyl flooring while her beautiful spare topper cake sat useless on the counter, she couldn't deliver the replacement cake until she received the green light from Kristi, Brady's sister.

Until tonight, Alicia hadn't realized Kristi Jacobs existed. After experiencing a sparkle of attraction with Brady last fall—which did not dovetail with her goals and dreams and plans in the slightest—she'd made it her mission to learn as little as possible about the sexy cop. He was too charming and therefore threatened her peace of mind.

For the foreseeable future, she intended to concentrate on Bitty Cakes. And she couldn't forget her long-held conviction not to let her heart stray anywhere near cop territory.

Everything had been going swimmingly, as her dear, departed Great-Aunt Gert would have said. Then, at the end of June, the Jacobs contract with another cupcakery fell through. The news sped to the Briarton Police Department, where Brady worked under her father's command. Alicia lived in and operated Bitty Cakes out of Rosevale, another Seattle suburb. Without her input—or her permission—Dad hinted Brady should recommend Bitty Cakes to his mom. Alicia could have refused the job, but that would have been an even more neurotic choice.

Her phone chimed a text alert. She scooped the

device off the stainless-steel counter. A message from Kristi!

Five minutes? the text read. *Still drying Mom's dress.*

Alicia gnawed the inside of her cheek. Five minutes sounded like an eternity.

Need help? she typed.

Kristi: *No. Everyone's having fun. Don't feel bad.*

Alicia's pinky finger twitched. *OK,* she keyed. But she did feel bad. It wasn't like her to stand idly by while Brady and his father and his sister *and* his mother took control of the situation.

"Hey, there," a deep male voice said. "Need help?"

Déjà vu-vu-vu. Alicia tucked her phone into her skirt pocket. Pressing a palm against the cool counter, she spun on her heels. Mr. Sexy and Sincere stood inside the kitchen, phone in hand. Brady's eyebrows cocked, and his luscious lips curved into a smile.

A sensuous sensation coursed through her. She ran a fingertip across a corner of her mouth. You know, to prevent the escape of drool.

"Oh. Hey. Why are you back here?"

"Thought I'd check on things." He indicated his phone. "I wanted to talk to you anyway, when Kristi texted that you were freaking out."

Alicia scoffed. "I'm not freaking out."

Brady pocketed his phone and stepped toward her. One little step. Nothing major. But her pulse jumped. Her breathing grew shallow. Secret parts of her body dampened.

Why, oh why, did Brady Jacobs affect her composure to such an alarming degree?

"Not freaking out," he echoed. "All right." His gaze veered to her hands. "You're wringing the life out of that dishrag."

Alicia stared at the cloth. When had she grabbed it?

She tossed the rag into the sink. "Okay, I'm a little restless. This party is my biggest catering event to date. I have to get it right."

"Who says you're not getting it right?"

At least twenty of his parents' guests. But she wouldn't mention the humiliating pictures and posts. "Brady, listen. I appreciate your part in getting me this job—"

"Your dad insisted. I respect the man and his opinions."

Of course. Everyone respected Alicia's father, who'd raised five children as a single parent after losing his wife to cancer. Alicia worshipped her dad, but she wasn't a confused and hurting little girl any longer. Or a teenager struggling to find her identity in a male-dominated household.

At twenty-six, she owned her dream business, because of her inheritance from her Great-Aunt Gert. Bitty Cakes was a testament to her deceased aunt *and* her mom. Both had been strong, independent women, and Alicia wanted to do their memories proud.

Her phone triple-dinged in her skirt. She flinched. Three notifications in a row couldn't be good.

Brady's gaze flew to her hip, and the device buzzed yet another social media alert.

His eyes danced. "Carrying concealed?"

"It's my phone, but not my text tone." In other words, not his sister sending a message to bring out the spare slicing cake. "Ignore it." Alicia placed a hand over her skirt pocket.

Brady chuckled. "Ignore your dinging, buzzing, secret-agent skirt. Yes, ma'am."

Heat swamped her neck. "What happened out

there—" She gestured at the door. "It's a catastrophe."

"It was an accident."

"I need to salvage my shop's reputation. And I can do that on my own." She needed to stay strong and keep erecting roadblocks against his steadfast sexiness.

He flipped up a hand. "I agree that cupcake virtuosos can manage damn near any disaster. But why should they need to do it all alone? Seems a shame." He pantomimed clasping an invisible microphone and holding the mic to his mouth. "One woman," he stated in a dramatic movie-trailer voice. "Three hundred guests. Downing champagne and gobbling cupcakes. A small child darts between the tables, dropping frosting and wreaking destruction. Can the cupcake master stop him? Or will he nap to thwart her another day?"

Alicia's lips twitched. "The adorable monster is asleep?"

Brady nodded. "On his mom's lap." He set aside the imaginary mic. "Alicia, your assistant let you down. Lying to get a job and then quitting when things go wrong? That sucks. Everything else is easily fixed."

"Oh, yeah? Like my speeding ticket?" *Whoops.*

Her eyes popped. The words had leaped out of her mouth.

Brady smiled. "Going there, are we?"

"No, no," she backpedaled. "I broke the law." Her dad had raised her to right her wrongs. "But you cited a lower speed on the ticket."

"I do have leeway on these occasions."

"You did a favor I didn't ask for."

"That's awful. I'm a horrible human being."

She fortified herself against his charming allure. "My dad wouldn't cut me slack for driving too fast."

Brady crossed his arms. "Your *dad* wasn't in the patrol car. You pleaded your case about not seeing the construction signs then practically begged me to slap on the handcuffs and drag you to the slammer."

The slapping-on-cuffs part didn't sound bad. And if he'd dragged her to his bed—

Don't go there. She pressed two fingertips to her temple. "I feel stupid for not seeing through her."

"Who?" Forehead furrowing, he stepped closer. "Lettie?"

Alicia nodded.

"Are we off the subject of the speeding ticket and back to your employee?"

"Yes." Anything to stop those errant thoughts about his bed—and his nearness. Her heart drummed. "Lettie was always a bit anxious in the kitchen. She enjoyed working up front, but that wasn't why I hired her. It didn't occur to me she wasn't truthful about her references or her kitchen skills." Alicia sounded naïve, but she knew what it felt like to want a chance so badly. She should be steaming mad at Lettie. Instead, she just wanted to move on.

"It sounds like you believe the best of people," Brady said in a sympathetic voice. "There's nothing wrong with that. But who'll help you clean this place after everyone leaves?"

Her chest tightened. "I don't know. My clerk is out of town this weekend. Bitty Cakes was closed today to allow preparation time for your parents' party."

"What about your friends?"

She shook her head. "It's too last-minute." Plus, they were recovering from last night's bachelorette extravaganza.

Her phone dinged. Resolve crumbling, she whipped out the device and waved it at Brady like a flag of surrender. "Look at these!"

He strode over. Accepting the phone, he studied the notifications. "People are talking about Bitty Cakes." He looked at her again.

"In a negative way!"

"Alicia. Hey." Compassion filled his deep voice. For an instant, she thought he might reach out, touch her hand. Her breathing quickened, but his gaze bent to the phone.

"Isn't all publicity good publicity?" he asked.

"Maybe in the olden days. Now, one misstep could force me to shut down."

He extended the phone toward her. "That's not happening. Lettie isn't hurt. She popped in on a thread to ease your mind. Some people think her tumble was funny. Yeah, there are troll comments, but most people say you handled the problems like a pro."

Alicia's heart pounded. "They do?"

He nodded, handing back the phone. They stood hip to hip, perusing the screen. As Alicia swiped post after post, her worry receded. There were plenty of snarky remarks. Still, between clips of Don and Maureen and the snippets of Lettie's confession, most of the comments weren't as atrocious as she'd feared.

Brady's upper arm grazed her shoulder. Darn it. She found the brief contact reassuring.

"These posts will hurt Lettie's reputation more than yours," he said.

For a youthful mistake? "Not if I can help it." Alicia stepped away and tapped out a couple of responses, asking people not to judge-and-jury Lettie. Everyone deserved a second chance, and Lettie would grow from her choices, although not as a Bitty Cakes employee. Alicia's sense of charity only went so far.

She sensed the weight of Brady's gaze on her face.

"What?" she asked, breathless again as their glances met. The man affected her like no one else.

Ever.

He smiled. "I see what you're doing, Alicia Maxwell. You have a good heart."

Her tummy warmed. "Ah. Um. Thank you."

He motioned toward the door. "We can ask everyone out there to put away their phones."

She shook her head. "People like to share their good times. It's not their fault if their good time is my bad time."

"That's a great way to look at it."

"Um. Ah. Thanks." Her phone chimed, and she scanned a text from his sister. Relief washed through her. "Your mom is ready for the slicing cake."

"Excellent. May I suggest something?"

Alicia stared at him. Wow, a man was *asking* if she wanted his opinion instead of inundating her with unsolicited advice? She put away her phone. "Go ahead."

He collected the cake from the counter. "Show everyone wielding their cameras how you respond under stress." He passed her the tray, and the tension slowly dissolved from her shoulders. And she had Brady to thank for helping her feel centered.

Minutes ago, in the hall, amid hundreds of partygoers, she'd said she could manage on her own. That hadn't changed. She *could*.

But maybe, for this one hectic night, it might not be a bad idea to let somebody in.

Not just anyone. Brady Jacobs. A potentially major distraction.

Should she risk letting him in?

Chapter Three

Sometime after midnight, Brady said goodbye to his cousins who'd chipped in with cleanup. They'd dismantled the dinner tables and stacked most of the chairs. The guys sauntered out of the building, laughing and joking. Alicia and Kristi chatted near the coat hooks. Alicia's gaze moved toward his. She lifted a finger as if to say, "I'll be there in a jiffy."

Brady gave her a glance and resumed stacking chairs. Not one guest from tonight's party would forget her poise and professionalism handling the slicing cake fiasco. Alicia was pretty and efficient, attentive and resourceful. He had every confidence her cupcake shop would succeed, hopefully beyond her wildest dreams. Was there room in her life for anything else?

Or anyone else?

Specifically, him?

Finally, Kristi waved goodbye over her shoulder and left with the last of their relatives. Only Brady and Alicia remained inside the hall. She stayed near the coat hooks another few moments, hands on her cheeks. Probably getting her bearings. It had been a long night.

Her smile a trifle wide to consider natural, she walked over. "Hey," she said, voice reverberating with deliberate casualness and palpable nerves. "I sent Kristi home. She's meeting a friend early tomorrow for a bike ride."

He nodded. "She enjoyed working with you tonight. I did too." He patted an unstacked chair. "Sit and rest. I'll finish the chairs. Or head home yourself," he offered, not wanting her to feel awkward with the guy she'd ghosted. "I can lock up and drop the keys by the bakery."

She smiled. "Sounds tempting, but I'm the hired help, Brady. Not you."

"Okay." He tamped down the urge to crow. "Then sit. Watch me strut my stuff. Maybe I'll impress you."

"You already have. So has your sister. Your whole family, really."

This was getting better and better. "We're a fun bunch. Come on. Sit."

Alicia dropped onto the chair. Fidgeted with her hands. Then leaped to her feet. "It'll go faster if we both stack."

Brady laughed. She was flustered. It was cute. *She* was cute. So damned appealing, his chest ached.

"You did a great job tonight," he said as they worked. The metal legs banged and echoed in the empty banquet hall. "This party was one for my family's record books. Everyone had a blast, and not a single cupcake crumb remained."

Her dark lashes swept downward. "Thank you. I couldn't have done it without you."

"Yeah, you could have."

She tucked two knuckles under her chin. A thoughtful furrow creased her forehead. Then a smile burst across her face. "You're right. I could have. It would have taken me a heck of a lot longer, though. So, again, thank *you*."

Brady chuckled. As they stacked, their hands brushed. Hers darted away as if she'd touched a scorching hot coal.

"Sorry," he said, although apologizing for the welcome contact was the last thing on his mind.

Alicia bent to clasp a chair. Her long hair fell over

her face, but he noted her tiny intake of breath, a sign she didn't see him as any old joe. She felt something when they were together. And that felt incredible.

"Alicia?" he whispered.

She lifted the chair between them. A polite smile perched on her lips. "Yes?"

"I know it's too late for anything tonight, but remember last fall when I asked you for coffee?"

Their gazes caught and held. A thrumming awareness zapped into his bones. Something inevitable about this woman called out to him. Reached *inside* him. Grabbed his heart and squished the suddenly mushy organ until he felt like he was tumbling. Down, down, down.

"I remember," she said softly.

"I was thinking I should ask again."

A shadow flitted over her face. "Brady, I like you, but..."

"It's okay. I can take a but."

"Well, I said it last fall, and I'll say it again. I don't date cops."

He bumped up one shoulder. "Thought I'd check on a policy update."

"It's the same." Blushing, she stacked her chair.

"To be clear," he persisted, "you're not against dating in general?"

"No." She laughed, and the melodious sound chimed in the big room. "I probably seem like a control freak, but I'm not talking to any guys right now. I haven't for months. Bitty Cakes is my life."

"And you have nothing against coffee itself." This Brady knew. They'd each drained mugs while packing supplies. But he wanted to stretch out these moments alone with her in the intimate emptiness of the banquet hall.

She shook her head, her blue gaze lively despite the late hour.

"You just don't date cops, regardless of whether or not they drink coffee."

Her lips twitched. "I don't date cops who drink tea."

"Any hope for hot chocolate?"

She smiled. "Nope."

"Let me guess. Too many badges in the family."

"You gotta admit, five is a lot."

"Good to know it's not me, then."

They exchanged a long glance, and she ran a hand through her dark hair. "It's not you," she whispered.

Brady hefted the final two chairs at once, his

objective set. At last, he'd met a woman who piqued his interest, and she slammed on the brakes because of his profession. He didn't want to push her into saying more. Not tonight, while they remained isolated in the party room.

"You're an enigma, Alicia Maxwell," he said, ending on a half-smile.

A puzzle he intended to solve.

On *her* terms, whatever they might be.

Two days later, Alicia transferred a dozen frosted cupcakes to the Bitty Cakes display case. With luck, this would be the last batch her new customers demanded. She was running low on supplies and energy.

Most weekdays, she woke early and whipped up six varieties of cupcakes in her shop around the corner from her apartment. Her flurry of morning baking usually sufficed until closing. But today's business eclipsed previous sales records. At three in the afternoon, just four flavors of tiny cakes remained, only because she'd increased production as the hours had passed. Otherwise, she might have needed to turn away some regulars, which wouldn't do.

Bitty Cakes had become known in the neighborhood for changing menu items throughout the week while also offering themed specials of the month. If a customer wanted a Monday cupcake, they needed to come by the cupcakery on Monday. Happily, today's options included the Minty Chippy flavor served at the Jacobs anniversary party Saturday night. The Chippy had been flying out of Alicia's ovens for hours.

She placed the last cupcake in the display case. "Cross your fingers the rush has passed," she murmured to Yuri, the counter attendant.

Yuri's dark eyebrows lifted. "The rush? It was more like a stampede."

"It was, wasn't it?" Alicia permitted herself a small smile. Her pulse raced as her thoughts drifted to how easily Brady had allayed her concerns about the social media posts Saturday night. To her relief, the response had been mainly positive. One video of his mom trying to catch the slicing cake had gone viral throughout Greater Seattle, prompting a morning text of praise from Maureen: No one will forget our party!

Yuri pointed to the vertical rows of glass in the

multi-paned storefront. "Alicia, look. Here comes your friend Lacey with Spats. Wasn't she walking the little buddy near your building today?"

Alicia lifted a shoulder. "You know how it goes. Lacey has a lot on her plate this week. I'm happy she can help with my dog at all." Alicia directed her gaze to the pane decorated with the Bitty Cakes logo. Lacey DeMarco, her good friend and across-the-hall neighbor, hitched Spats to a pole in the shaded doggy parking area under the awning. Like other businesses on the dog-friendly block, Bitty Cakes followed public health regulations while allowing owners to keep an eye on their fur-babies.

Yuri dug colored chalk markers out of a drawer. "Walking your dog will make a nice break."

"Are you volunteering for the job?" Alicia teased, glimpsing Spats lapping from the communal water bowl she cleaned each morning. Early last winter, she'd inherited the ten-year-old dachshund from her Great-Aunt Gert, along with the cash to open her shop. Caring for the senior Doxie kept her hopping but also filled her life with joy.

Yuri grinned. "I wish I could walk Spats. It's a beautiful afternoon. But I've had two breaks today. You've been on your feet since dawn."

Alicia pressed a palm to the apron covering her

top. "Yuri, I need to keep you happy. If you quit on me, I'd be lost."

"Oh, Alicia. I love working here, and you're a wonderful boss. You'll find someone reliable to replace Lettie. Don't stress." Yuri commenced updating the menu board.

"I hope so."

The shop bell tinkled, and Lacey entered. Alicia moved out from behind the display case and greeted her friend with a hug.

Lacey swiped a blond wisp of hair off her forehead. "Hey, Alicia. Sorry I can't walk Spats today."

"That's okay." Alicia often found time to go home following her pet's noon nap and walk Spats from there. On other days, Lacey, who created lingerie designs from a studio in her apartment, took over. "You're as busy as I am."

Lacey twirled a hand. "Walking your dog gets my head out of my designs, but right now is hurry-hectic." She sat at a small table near the window and tucked her purse by her sandals.

"I have everything crossed for you with Clemmons Consulting," Alicia said, twining two fingers. "Can I tempt you with a moist and delicious bitty cake before you go?" She was pretty sure she knew the answer. Lacey often taste-tested her new recipes.

Lacey's eyes brightened. "You had me at moist. Is there any Triple Coconut left?"

"Precisely one. We'll share."

Alicia returned to the display case and donned compostable food-service gloves. Stepping around Yuri, she sliced the Triple Coconut into quarters and arranged the pieces on a plate. After removing her gloves and apron, she returned to Lacey's table, set down the cupcake and two glasses of lemonade. She spotted Spats, nose squished against a low pane of glass, contributing to the row of canine nostril art she or Yuri wiped off throughout the day. The dog's floppy ears perked.

"Just a second," Alicia said to Lacey, fishing a homemade dog treat from a pocket of her Capri pants. "Spats has that sweet, pleading look."

Lacey wiggled her fingers at the pooch. "When doesn't he have that look?"

Chuckling, Alicia went outside. "Hey, boy. I can't pet you right now. In a few minutes, okay? On our walk." She dangled the cookie in front of his nose. "Sit like a good little guy."

Spats sat on the shaded part of the sidewalk. His front paws stretched.

"Super spiffy Spats," Alicia murmured in the tender tone the dog adored. She broke apart the treat between his paws. "I won't be long."

Spats munched, oblivious to the world outside his snack.

Back inside, Alicia washed her hands at the counter sink before sitting down with Lacey. "How are preparations for your presentation going?" she asked, pushing the Bitty Cakes plate toward her friend.

Lacey picked up a quarter of the cupcake featuring a rich, gooey center. A thick swirl of frosting and toasted coconut flakes topped the Triple. "It's a lot of work, but I'm giving this meeting everything I have." Lacey sampled the cupcake. "Yum. Derek is helping me."

"Yum for the Triple or yum for Derek?" Derek McAllister was Lacey's new boyfriend, since Friday night.

Lacey winked. "Yum-*yum* for both."

Alicia's eyebrows climbed. "Oh? Are you modeling designs for him?"

"In a way. He pretends to be a venture capitalist, and I act out the presentation following his shift." Lacey's lips curved.

"Aw. I'm happy for you." Derek, the twin brother

of another close friend, was a nice guy. He and Alicia saw each other a few times before her great-aunt passed. And more than a year before Brady entered the picture.

Not that Brady was *in* the picture, she reminded herself, suppressing a flash of impatience. She needed to shake off this lingering Brady fog. She couldn't go the distance—she couldn't even attempt the romantic equivalent of the hundred-yard-dash—with any guy right now, never mind a man as compelling as Brady. She needed to stay focused on building Bitty Cakes.

"Derek is off the market, huh?" She forced a playful tone.

Lacey devoured a second quarter of the cupcake. "You bet he is. You missed a good man there, Alicia." Lacey licked a dollop of filling off her thumb and studied the remaining portions on the plate. "You *are* okay that he and I are dating, right?"

"More than okay. Janie made sure of it before she set you two up."

"I'm not complaining. Really, I should thank you for having a rule about not dating cops. Otherwise, you and Derek might still be a thing."

"We were never a thing. We just talked a few times to satisfy Janie."

"But you're allergic to dating the boys in blue. Or so you claim."

"I don't claim. I follow through." Alicia sipped her lemonade. "It's difficult for me to separate the man from the job." She picked at coconut flakes on the plate.

Lacey's head angled. "In what way?"

Alicia chose a piece of the Triple before turning the plate toward her friend again. "I don't want to scare you away from Derek—"

"Believe me, my friend, that's not happening."

Alicia sighed. "Well, being a police officer comes with a host of complexities." She broke apart her cupcake portion and ate a small chunk. "The call-outs outside rostered hours had a huge effect on me when I was a kid. The disappointment when my dad couldn't make my piano recitals was soul-crushing. Other family plans got canceled at the last minute, and my mom wasn't there to help balance things out." The emotional stress and inherent dangers of police work had worried Alicia that her dad's life could end any second. But she wouldn't describe those childhood fears to Lacey. She nibbled more cupcake. "Growing up in the life doesn't mean I want to marry into it. So why even start down that path with a guy?"

"Why allow yourself to feel a teensy bit tempted?" Lacey pushed.

A wave of regret swelled beneath Alicia's breastbone. But not regarding Derek. About *Brady*.

She wiped her hands on a paper napkin. "Something like that."

"I get it," Lacey responded. "Alicia, I do. You're coming at relationships from an entirely different headspace. For me, now that I've met Derek, it's another ball game. Before, I was all about work. Like you."

"Before you met Derek *Friday night*, you mean?" Alicia joked to lighten her mood. Not three days had passed since the bachelorette party, and Lacey sounded like she and Derek had paired up for life.

"I know it sounds fast," Lacey said. "It *is* fast. I'm not sure I could resist that man, no matter the circumstances. It's like there's this,"—Lacey held out her hands, pushing and pulling air—"gigantic magnet between us, you know?"

Alicia nodded as if she understood. But she hadn't experienced a magnetic pull with any of her old boyfriends. Just pleasant tugs. Her reasons for not dating cops aside, when it came right down to it, she wanted the pull. She craved the pull. She *deserved* the pull.

"You and Derek are a great fit," she reassured her friend.

"I agree." Lacey dusted crumbs off her palms. "Before I go, during my limited free time this morning, I investigated your weekend shenanigans." She accessed a social media site on her phone. "Alicia, tell me, who is the sweet slice of mystery man in these pictures? His hand is on your arm in this one." Lacey slid the device across the table. "He looks awestruck, and you're glowing."

Alicia's pulse accelerated. Oh, God, it appeared Brady *was* in the picture. As in, the digital gem shining from a mutual acquaintance's social feed.

In the post, Alicia and Brady stood near the dessert table at his parents' anniversary party while his parents fed each other cake. Alicia recalled the interaction in vivid detail. A guest had jostled her, and for a moment Brady's hand had indeed rested on her arm. Her skin had pebbled. Her face had heated. She'd caught her lower lip between her teeth like a character in a cheesy movie.

Worse, she'd dreamed about the tantalizing pressure of Brady's touch throughout Saturday night.

Also, Sunday night. As in, last night.

In her dreams, he'd caressed her body in places other than her socially acceptable arm.

"That's Brady Jacobs," she informed Lacey in a weird, squeaky voice. "My dad is his commander at the Briarton PD."

"Interesting." Lacey tapped her fingernails on the table. "Then Brady Jacobs is a cop?"

"Um." Alicia paused. "Yeah."

"And, therefore, he's off-limits?"

"To me?" Alicia asked, hunching her shoulders.

Lacey glanced around the shop. "I don't see anyone else at this table."

Er. Um. "Then yerse."

"*Yerse?*" Lacey parroted. "You're saying Brady Jacobs *is* off-limits? '*Yes*' is the word I'm looking for." Lacey's eyes sparkled.

"Yerse," Alicia mumbled as a spasm clenched the bridge of her nose. The sensation felt as bizarre as it probably appeared. Damn it, why couldn't she say yes? The word contained one short, snappy syllable. Brady Jacobs *was* off-limits. Some other lucky woman would land Mr. Sexy and Sincere.

Lacey reached for her phone. "Jealousy isn't a good look on you, Alicia."

"If Brady is off-limits, why would I feel jealous?"

"My question exactly."

Alicia scrunched her nose. A man and woman entered the shop, and she reassembled her features into a professional mask as the duo placed an order, which Yuri quickly filled. The couple left, chatting and cuddling.

Alicia leaned forward, confiding in Lacey. "If you must know, Brady helped me Saturday night after the party," she said in a quiet tone that wouldn't carry to Yuri behind the display case, fifteen feet away. "So did his sister and some of their cousins. We stacked chairs and drank coffee. It was no big deal."

"The pink on your face says otherwise."

"You can't trust the pink on my face."

"I believe I can."

"*Lacey.*"

Her friend's glance flitted to the window. "Alicia, don't look." Lacey shielded her gaze with a hand, looking for all the world like an inquisitive sailor eyeing a horizon. "Your Brady is petting Spats," she half-whispered.

"What? He's here? In Rosevale?" Alicia stared at the remains of their shared cupcake. "And he's not *my* Brady."

"Not yet, he isn't. He's reading the name of the shop," Lacey whispered. "By the way, he's in uniform. My, that's a nice, shiny badge."

The bell above the shop door jingled, and the back of Alicia's neck tingled. She fought the urge to glance over her shoulder and thirstily drink him in. Or offer to serve him, which wasn't necessary and sounded naughty. She was on break. In a cupcakery. Yuri could handle his needs—as a customer.

"I don't require a play-by-play," she whispered, shrinking down further in her chair. Except, in her small shop, what would her silly ostrich act accomplish?

"Shh," Lacey whispered. "He's ordering something." Lacey gaped. "The man asked for *two dozen* salted caramel cupcakes. Do you have that many?"

"Yes," Alicia mumbled. "Fresh from the ovens. And I can hear him as easily as you can." As Brady spoke to Yuri, his deep, friendly voice floated across the shop, slipped beneath her skin, and snuggled around, making itself at home.

"He's looking over here," Lacey whispered, squirming on her chair. "He's spotting you."

"Oh, for—" Alicia sat up. She couldn't hide from the man. Clasping the back of her chair, she turned.

Brady tipped his police hat. "Hey, there."

Alicia's heart spasmed. Forget her nose! Her

most important internal organ lurched and squeezed at the sight of Brady Jacobs.

"Oh, no," she whispered. "Oh, no, no, no, no, no." She whirled to face Lacey.

"What?" her friend whispered.

Alicia gulped. *"The pull."*

Chapter Four

Brady gazed at Alicia sitting at the small table with her friend. Her head swung toward him a second time, her blue eyes round and her dark brows lifted. Her lashes swept up and then slowly down. She blinked.

She looked dazed. Yeah, that was the word. Or, more accurately, stunned.

Great. He'd uttered a casual greeting, and the woman he yearned to ask out on one simple date resembled a shoplifter caught stuffing mascara packages into her purse. Did his interest in Alicia Maxwell radiate off him in tangible waves? And it— what? Scared her? Annoyed her? Was she formulating another way to brush him off?

He took off his police hat and slipped the brim beneath his arm. "Nice to see you again." He smiled.

Alicia's mouth fell open. Not a single word emerged.

Her friend jumped up, eyes on her phone. "Look at the time. I gotta run." The woman rushed out the door without sparing a glance at the small dog parked beneath the awning.

"Wait! Your dog—" Brady caught the door before it closed. "Hold on to those cupcakes," he called to the clerk boxing his order. Alicia's friend hoofed it down the sidewalk and disappeared into the flow of pedestrians.

Releasing a breath, he stepped into the shop again. Alicia rose from her chair. "Your friend forgot her dog?" he asked, guessing—

"Spats isn't Lacey's," Alicia confirmed. "He's mine."

"Spats," he repeated. "Like those old-time spatter guards for protecting shoes. That's a cute name." Alicia and the little dog made an enchanting pair.

"He's a dachshund," she responded with a blush. "His name isn't a product of my rusty imagination, I'm afraid to say. I, uh, got him from a relative." Her gaze roamed around the bakery, avoiding his face. *And* his badge, he realized.

Warmth spread throughout his body as he added two plus two. Alicia wasn't immune to his interest. No, she returned it. She might not want to, but she did.

"I'm sorry," she said, shaking her head as if her thoughts spun in a million directions. "I need to walk Spats, then get back to work. We've been incredibly busy. Haven't we, Yuri?" She looked at the clerk, who'd placed his order to the side of the till.

The woman she'd called Yuri nodded. "We're missing a team member, which I suppose you know, Officer Jacobs."

The warmth inside Brady's chest deepened. He and Yuri hadn't formally met, but if Alicia and the clerk were friends as well as boss and employee, either Alicia had described her time with him Saturday night or Yuri had identified him from the online pictures and videos.

"You've seen the posts from my parents' anniversary party?" he asked.

Yuri's friendly brown eyes shone with good humor. "Half of the Pacific Northwest has seen the videos of your mom trying to catch the slicing cake.

Names were tagged. I'll admit, I watched my share of clips."

Brady rubbed his jaw. "Yeah, I don't know why my mom jumped toward the dessert."

Yuri chuckled. "Instinct. She was protecting cake. Anyway, Alicia posted an ad for Lettie's job yesterday. We've had seventy-eight applicants. In one day! Isn't that fantastic?"

Alicia flicked him a glance. "I need to comb over their references. I can't afford another disaster."

"Boss," Yuri chided. "Sales are out of this world. Celebrate your success."

"The publicity from the videos worked," Alicia said. "More eyes are on Bitty Cakes. One blunder can be funny. Repeats are another matter."

"Foodies would have discovered this place soon enough," Brady noted. "The videos sped up the process. Alicia, your baking is delicious." Mouth-watering scents filled the shop, teasing his nostrils and tantalizing his taste buds. The aromas couldn't compare to the beguiling sight of Alicia Maxwell, though. She wore a short-sleeved top in the same shade of pale blue as the logo painted on the window. Fashionable sailor pants completed her outfit. His mom or sister would recall the correct term. He appreciated the style, which revealed a flash of leg.

Yuri's gaze ping-ponged between him and Alicia.

Brady stepped toward the clerk. "Yuri, I'm Brady Jacobs. The internet is ahead of me, but Alicia catered my parents' anniversary party this weekend."

"Nice to meet you. I'm Yuri Sato." Smiling, she removed her food-service gloves, and they shook hands over the curved-front display case.

Alicia groaned. "Where are my manners? Yuri, this is Brady. Brady, please meet Yuri."

"We've got it covered," Brady kidded.

Yuri gestured at Brady's Briarton PD badge. "At first, I didn't recognize you from your mother's videos. You weren't in uniform. To be honest, I watched more of Lettie's clips. So I was curious what a Briarton officer was doing in Rosevale. Now I know."

Brady offered his pleasant-cop smile. "What can I say? Alicia's father brought in a box of red velvet cupcakes one day, and the Briarton PD got hooked." *He* was hooked. On Alicia Maxwell.

He turned his gaze to the woman who'd captivated him for months. Their moments alone in the banquet hall kitchen Saturday night and then afterward, cleaning up, had convinced him he wanted more. His dad had said maybe Alicia hadn't met the right cop. Brady wanted the chance to prove he was the right *man* for her, regardless of his job. But she was skittish—with a capital S. He intended to move things along at a sloth's pace before analyzing the results.

"Where do you walk Spats?" he asked, glancing at her dog staring in the bakery window. The dachshund leaped around on a short leash and barked.

Alicia made eye contact with the pooch. She held up a finger, and the animal settled.

"There's a dog run two blocks away," she replied, looking at Brady. "Spats needs to go do his thing." She stepped toward the door. "And I need to take him there."

"The fenced-in green space by the library?" He asked.

Alicia's blue eyes sparkled. "That's the one."

"Mind if I tag along?" Brady put on his Briarton PD hat. "My sister Kristi volunteers at that library. She wants to answer your ad but asked if I would check in with you first, seeing as you and I share some history. She doesn't want to spring her application on you or make you feel obligated."

"Your sister wants Lettie's job?" Alicia asked, surprise threading her tone.

Brady acknowledged the question with a nod. "Kristi enjoys organizing parties. Baking, cooking, decorating. All that stuff. She has event-planning experience and worked for a Tacoma catering company. Her references are legit." He sounded like a human billboard touting his sister's accomplishments, but if doing Kristi this favor granted him more time with Alicia, he was onboard.

Alicia glanced at Yuri. "Kristi is the person I told you about earlier. She was a great help Saturday night."

The clerk smiled. "Alicia, after what happened with Lettie, hiring someone you know sounds perfect."

"I don't know her well. I know Brady. And their mom."

"But an officer under your dad's command vouches for Kristi," Yuri persisted. "That seems timely."

"It's your lucky day," Brady said to Alicia.

She gnawed her lip. "It couldn't hurt to talk to Kristi, I guess."

Yuri swept her hands toward the exit. "You two go ahead. Discuss the job opening. Officer Jacobs, I'll keep your order behind the counter until you return."

"Thanks." He glanced at Alicia. "Then it's settled?" He opened the bakery door to the beautiful summer day. And, perhaps, to a new future for his sister and himself.

"A walk and a talk," Alicia replied, heading for her dog. "Then we'll see."

Alicia needed to make a smart decision. The future of Bitty Cakes was at stake. She'd thought she'd checked off every box hiring Lettie, and look how that experience had turned out. So what the heck was she doing, agreeing to an on-the-fly interview with Brady's sister?

She and the attractive police officer strolled along the sidewalk toward the library and the adjoining green space with an enclosed dog run. Spats stopped at the base of full-leafed trees, sniffing interesting places. Shoppers and tourists crowded the wide walkways and browsed the picturesque shops. A temperate breeze drifted in the baby-blue sky dotted with cotton-puff clouds.

Spats picked up the pace, slipping between

Brady and Alicia to trot his I'm-in-charge Doxie stuff. Brady slid his phone into a pocket of his police pants and greeted an elderly pedestrian before turning his dazzling gaze on Alicia. "All set. Kristi is meeting us at the dog park in ten."

"Sounds good."

"Thanks for agreeing to talk to her. And please, no pressure about hiring my little sister. Kristi understands you need to do what's best for Bitty Cakes."

A corner of Alicia's mouth tugged up. What was best for Bitty Cakes was a clone of herself. As efficient as Kristi had been Saturday night, Alicia required an employee who could work unsupervised, allowing the business to accept more catering gigs. Kristi's potential cupcake duties included a lot more than baking or serving customers when Yuri wasn't on shift.

The warm breeze swished her hair, and Alicia swept a thick strand off her face. "If Kristi is a good fit, I won't need to pore over those dozens and dozens of applications. I'll still need to at least look at them." What if the perfect candidate sat at her digital fingertips? Or what if she hired Kristi and the experience soured? Would Officer Brady ever get the urge to, um, ticket Alicia again?

He smiled. "Not to influence you, but my mom handed out twenty-nine of your business cards at her yoga class yesterday. Good thing she asked for the entire pack in your purse."

Alicia gasped. She had given Maureen fifty cards! "Wow. I'll text her a thanks. A call came in this morning about catering a sixteenth birthday party in a couple of weeks. Was that because of your mom?"

"If the caller was Helen Blankenship, yes."

"That's awesome." Grinning, Alicia adjusted her grip on Spats's leash. "Except a friend is getting married the same day. I'm a bridesmaid. I can't tack on the Blankenship party."

"Can Yuri handle the birthday? She seems great."

Alicia sighed. "Yuri is wonderful, but she has a family commitment. It's the middle of the summer, and she's working extra hours until I replace Lettie. I won't ask her to take more time away from her husband and kids."

Spats crossed the sidewalk in front of them to sniff a familiar yellow Labrador and the Lab's human. Alicia swapped the leash to her right hand and said hello to her fellow dog lover. After a few moments, the Lab barked, urging his human forward, and the group parted.

Alicia and Brady continued walking. Their upper arms brushed. Alicia's pulse skipped, and her cheekbones tingled. Her reaction to this man was unreal.

"Did you turn down Helen's party?" Brady asked, picking up their conversation.

"Not yet. She asked me to think outside of the box after I explained about the wedding. I don't know what else I can do, but she and I will touch base tomorrow."

Brady's eyes creased with a smile, and his head tipped. "It sounds to me like you need an employee who can start as soon as possible. Someone reliable and creative. Perchance someone who has a brother with recent experience handling cupcake disasters? Kristi is perfect."

"Perchance?" Alicia responded with a laugh. She liked Brady's wit. "Are you saying if I hired your sister, *you* would help her with the Blankenship sweet sixteen?" She pictured Brady monitoring two dozen teenagers and pitching in as he looked out for his younger sister. And looked out for Alicia's best interests, it seemed.

"I'm saying it's not out of the question. I'm free that day." The brim of his police hat shaded his gaze from the sun as he nodded. "Yeah, if my sister is your employee, I'll volunteer as her assistant. It'll be fun."

Alicia feigned offense. "Why, Officer Jacobs, is this a bribe to get Kristi the job?"

He stared ahead. "Never."

"Mm-hm." Oh, boy. Hiring Kristi Jacobs sounded more and more appealing. It also sounded dangerous—to Alicia's heart. If Kristi met the qualifications for working at Bitty Cakes, only Alicia's growing attraction to Brady stood in the way of locking in a dependable new employee.

Could she handle having the hots for a staff member's brother? How close were Kristi and Brady? Would Brady 'pop by for cupcakes' until Alicia either agreed to go for coffee or needed to date someone else to—hopefully—get him out of her mind?

None of those questions were appropriate for *this* discussion.

"Where does Kristi work now?" she asked instead. Spats strutted toward the dog park, and she followed her pet's lead.

"She's between jobs," Brady replied, hands clasped behind his exquisite posterior.

Since when did Alicia find cop uniforms sexy? Aside from three weeks ago, when Officer Jacobs stopped her for speeding...

"She was a server at O'Toole's," the man in question continued.

A red flag shot up. In the nick of time. *Whew.*

"Isn't O'Toole's the pub that lost its liquor license for serving underage?"

He cleared his throat. "Kristi wouldn't serve underage. It happened twice when she wasn't there. My sister likes to have a good time, but she's also a stickler for rules."

Hmm. Was he also describing himself? "Your parents don't strike me as sticklers." Don and Maureen Jacobs both seemed pretty laid back.

"You're right. They're not." He grinned. "Kristi and I rebelled."

Alicia couldn't stop a smile from spreading across her face. Neither could she prevent her thoughts from meandering down a romantic pathway. The questions peppered her mind and clouded her vision. So sue her for being curious.

Like, was Brady a stickler in bed—in a good way? When he kissed a girl...on the mouth...or in other locations...did he take his time? Was he, um, swift beneath the sheets, or did he prefer to examine, say, an entire body of evidence?

Her torso heated beneath her Bitty Cakes T-shirt.

"After what happened at O'Toole's," he explained, "Kristi took a week to think about her future before beginning another job search. With you and Bitty Cakes, she feels like the perfect opportunity has fallen in her lap."

"That's nice to hear." Much better than learning she'd come across like a cranky crone.

Spats let out a series of excited barks as they neared their destination, and Alicia looked toward the dog run, her gaze locating Brady's sister. Kristi stood beneath a large oak tree, wearing a cute skirt and top and holding a big plastic container. The younger woman waved, and Alicia and Brady waved back.

Brady leaned toward Alicia, his voice a husky timbre. "I wouldn't say this is fate or anything," he murmured in a manner indicating he believed it was, "but an optimist like my dad would say Kristi and I entered your life...for different reasons...at a very opportune time."

An optimist like his *dad*, huh? "Go on," Alicia responded, another smile curving her mouth.

"My sister wants a change, and she loves to bake. As you're about to learn when you taste her sample treats, she's amazing at it. She creates her own recipes."

Spats lunged toward the dog run, and Alicia tightened her grip on the leash. Kristi sounded too good to be true, and Brady's undeniable sexiness would test her sanity. And maybe also her romantic boundaries.

Was she ready for that?

"Kristi can help with the Blankenship party and the extra business coming your way," Brady said. "Why not trial her? No strings attached."

"I'll feel bad if it doesn't work out."

"If it works out, keep in mind that my family is close. It stands to reason you'd see more of me."

"I would?" Unbidden anticipation bubbled in her veins.

He slipped her one of his remarkable smiles. "I'd have to visit the bakery now and then to make sure my sister is holding up her end of the bargain by being a fantastic employee."

"Following that logic, if it doesn't work out, I *wouldn't* see more of you?" Alicia's ears burned. Why did she blurt inane statements around this guy? Had her brain abandoned its pathway to her mouth?

"Well, now." He paused, smile broadening. "That, Alicia, is entirely up to you."

Chapter Five

If Brady kept eating six cupcakes a day, he'd resemble a giant marshmallow man before he convinced Alicia to take a chance on him. The scariest part? He was cool with that.

As he entered Bitty Cakes Tuesday afternoon, he vowed not to blimp out on cupcakes during today's visit. He'd restrict himself to three of Alicia's tasty goodies. At most.

He swept his gaze around the bakery. Couples sat at the few tables, and a multitude of customers stood in line, chatting and waiting for service. Alicia —the sweetest treat in the place—plus Kristi and Yuri swapped turns at the cash register. The trio managed not to collide while passing out cupcakes and talking to the animated patrons.

The mouth-watering scent of fresh baking wafted in the crowded space. From across the shop, Alicia's gaze rose to meet his, and she smiled. The bright wattage of their connection heated him through.

Man, he *liked* this woman. Her powerful will and sense of purpose were catnip to a guy who'd dated ladies attracted to the shiny lure of a badge...and not much else. Those relationships had been fun, but he needed more.

Someday he wanted to dance at *his* thirtieth wedding anniversary. To feed his cherished wife cake. To gaze out at a throng of supportive friends and relatives and experience deep fulfillment.

For months he'd tried to shake off the feeling that Alicia Maxwell was a gateway to his future. How much longer could he ignore gut instinct?

He took his place in line. Several people glanced over their shoulders. Murmurs ensued as folks glimpsed his Briarton PD uniform. A middle-aged man motioned him ahead.

"Thanks, but I have plenty of time before my shift," Brady replied. He had arrived at Bitty Cakes two hours early, the same as yesterday.

The fellow shrugged. "At least it's not a Rosevale PD officer slacking off."

At least it wasn't a doughnut joke. "Like I said, plenty of time."

"Hey," commented a woman, tapping the bow of her upper lip as she joined in with the good-natured fun. "I saw you in a video online. You weren't in uniform."

A younger woman next to the lip-tapper asked, "Wasn't it your parents who had the cupcake tumble at their anniversary?"

Brady nodded. A precise, professional motion. "There was a minor incident, but I assure you, the cupcakes tasted as fantastic then as they smell today." He sounded wooden, but modulating his voice and body language went with the job. He rested his palms on his duty belt.

"Bitty Cakes is fabulous," the younger woman responded. "The funny video brought me here. The cupcakes keep me coming back."

Alicia looked up from filling an order, and Brady met her gaze again as a rosy color blossomed on her cheeks. She murmured something to his sister, and Kristi glanced around the crowd.

"Pay my handsome brother no mind, folks," Kristi called above the chatter. "No letting him butt in. He can wait in line like everyone else."

"Can *I* cut in front of him?" a young guy standing

behind Brady asked.

"That's no problem," Kristi returned.

Various folks in the shop laughed.

Kristi and Alicia exchanged amused glances.

"You heard her," Alicia informed the customers. "The Briarton officer waits. Now, if a Rosevale cop shows up, that's another matter."

The crowd laughed again and clapped. Someone whooped. Several patrons stepped in front of Brady, and Alicia's gaze shifted to his once more. A wide smile brightened her face, and he suppressed a chuckle.

The rush thinned as he reached the counter. Yuri moved out from the display case to collect dishes and sweep the floor, leaving Brady alone with Alicia and Kristi, aside from a couple on his right discussing the menu board.

Kristi's eyebrows lifted. "Hi, big bro. Are you checking up on me on my first day? Your confidence in my abilities is astounding."

"That's one reason I'm here," Brady ribbed. His sister fit right in with Alicia and Yuri, considering the sociable way the three women interacted.

Yesterday, Alicia offered to trial Brady's little sister for a month. The solution covered Bitty Cakes for the Blankenship sweet sixteen party and saved

Alicia from interviewing the flood of applicants for Lettie's job. Plus, the arrangement allowed Kristi the chance to shine in a role she enjoyed. There were no losers in this scenario.

Alicia slid him the side-eye. "You're checking up on Kristi? You mean to say you didn't stop in because you crave my cupcakes?"

"I definitely crave your cakes." He could gobble her up—uh, devour her cakes—every day. "I'm under orders to bring another two dozen cupcakes to the Briarton PD, if you can spare that many."

"Hmm." Her gaze narrowed. "This isn't my dad's doing, is it?"

"Nope." Since his time with Alicia Saturday night, Brady had realized it was super important to her that her father not interfere—too much—in her life. He couldn't imagine a dynamic man like his commander stepping back altogether.

He clarified, "The briefing sergeant asked for an order of Bitty Cakes, and I volunteered. Your father said something along the lines that it wasn't up to him. He and your brothers have stuffed your nest with enough twigs and grass that it's a wonder you're not choking on the stuff. It's time they let you wobble out onto a branch and fly. *His* words, not mine."

"Uh-huh," she commented.

"Or splat onto the ground," he tacked on. "That was the gist."

Alicia laughed. "Give me a second."

After talking to Kristi, she passed through a door into the kitchen. Two minutes later, she returned.

"The Pineapple Cherry cupcakes are cooling," she told Kristi. "The Chocolate Peanut Butters need chocolate sauce drizzled onto the frosting. This morning's batch was flawless."

"You got it," Kristi answered.

Brady's stomach rumbled, reminding him of his assignment. He looked at Alicia. "The Chocolate Peanut Butters sound great. I'll take a dozen of those and twelve of the Pineapple Cherry."

She nodded. "We have enough." She opened a Bitty Cakes box and lined the inside with decorative paper.

"Excellent." He waited a beat. "Is your friend bringing by your dog again? It's a beautiful day for another walk."

Alicia slid him an unhurried look, and he crossed his fingers behind his back.

Was she changing her mind about hanging out with a guy who wore the uniform of Those She

Dared Not Date? Or was she entertaining the notion of someday soon altering her stance?

"Spats is napping in my office," she responded, voice airy. "Want to sneak a couple of cupcakes from your order and go see him?"

Brady resisted the urge to sit back on his heels and beg. "With you?"

Her lips quirked. "Well, I can't allow you to wander the premises on your own. I might wind up with a cupcake heist on my hands. No offense."

"That's right," Yuri said, returning to the checkout. "Only authorized personnel and their guests permitted."

"Sounds fair." Unless Alicia used the time to warn him off again. But no risk, no reward.

Alicia collected two chocolate peanut butter cupcakes from the dwindling supply in the display case. "Coffee?" she asked, plating the desserts and tugging off her food-service gloves.

Kristi chuckled. "He always wants coffee. I'll bring in mugs."

"Thanks," Alicia responded to his sister. She crooked a finger over her shoulder. "This way, Officer Jacobs."

"Yes, ma'am." Brady stuck his hat beneath an arm. Kristi and Yuri giggled.

Brady trailed Alicia through a second door beside the kitchen. Paint the same soft shade of blue as her top coated both doors. His gaze dipped to her swaying hips as she carried the plates along a windowless corridor. He checked out her apron bow nestled above her perky rear. Swearing beneath his breath, he fixed his gaze on her upper back. Sexy shoulder blades moved beneath her top.

Yup. Sexy *shoulder blades*. He had it bad.

Needing a diversion, he squinted at an exit sign at the far end of the hall. They reached a Dutch door split in the middle, the bottom half shut and the upper half open. Spats napped burrowed into a small blanket on a dog bed in the leg space of an antique-looking rolltop desk. An oak swivel chair sat to one side, allowing the dog to explore the brick-walled office while confining the animal from the kitchen and customer areas.

"Hey, buddy," Alicia murmured to her pet. She set one plate on the wide top frame of the bottom door and twisted the knob. "Want company, Spatsy-Poo?"

The dog's head lifted. Spats yawned, emitted a yip, and stretched his front legs, dragging an object out from the fuzzy blanket.

Brady and Alicia entered the office.

"What's under his paw?" Brady asked, retrieving his plate.

She closed the door's lower half. "Lacey sewed Spats a teddy bear from her lingerie scraps." She slid a wood writing surface from a space above the left bottom bank of drawers. She gestured at Brady to put his plate on the pullout. Hers went on the main desktop. "Spats loves Boo-Bear. It's the one toy he doesn't chew to death. He just sucks it, like a lollipop."

Brady's throat constricted. "Sucks it?" Couldn't she have used another word?

A smile curved her mouth. "I'll admit it. My dog is into underwear. Did I mention yesterday that Lacey is a designer?"

"Of underwear?" Brady scratched his Adam's apple above his uniform collar. "I don't think you did."

"Well, she is. Don't worry, the scraps are clean. Spats isn't kinky."

"To each his own." Man, this conversation sparked sexy visuals he shouldn't let anywhere near his brain when he and Alicia hadn't gone on a single date. For instance, was she wearing one of her friend's lingerie designs beneath her apron, the blue top, and her sassy sailor pants? Or did she prefer sensible white cotton undies? Or—his mouth dried —*nothing?*

Did Alicia dig guys who dug women who wore lingerie? Maybe cute bras with ruffled bows. Or silky panties with slippery strings on the hips.

His body tightened below his belt, and he swallowed. She retrieved a dog biscuit from a compartment in the desk, sat on the swivel chair, and presented the treat to Spats. The dog bolted from his cushion and grabbed the cookie. Abandoning Boo-Bear, Spats scuttled to another bed in a corner and gnawed his prize.

Brady positioned the guest chair a foot from Alicia's and sat down. With his Department-issued footwear planted on the hardwood, he placed aside his hat and adjusted the weight of his duty belt. He imagined a punk launching a rock at his crotch, and the circumstances in his pants subsided.

His sister materialized at the split door. "Here you go." Kristi perched two coffee mugs on the bottom ledge. "Black for my brother, and a splash of cream for my new boss. I hope I remembered that correctly, Alicia."

"You did," Alicia replied, getting up and grabbing the mugs. "Thank you."

"Enjoy." Kristi left.

The rich scent of dark roast curled in the air as Alicia handed Brady his coffee. Their knees knocked when she sat back down, and their gazes reconnected. Hers appeared wary again now that they'd dispensed with the not-so-sordid tale of Spats's tastes in chew toys.

Brady sipped his hot brew as silence swelled between them. They had reached an awkward impasse. He liked Alicia Maxwell. A lot. And she liked him, but something held her back.

His people-reading skills honed on the job told him she hadn't invited him into her private space to be polite. She could have passed along his cupcake order to Kristi or Yuri and busied herself in the kitchen. But she hadn't.

The way he saw it, either Alicia Maxwell aimed to slice-and-dice his romantic prospects with a metaphorical machete or tell him she wasn't against dating *Brady Jacobs* in particular.

Or let him know she hadn't finished weighing her options.

His decision? To accept whatever cupcake crumbs she flicked his way.

For now, he just needed to get her talking again.

"This is a great piece of furniture," he said, smoothing a hand over the surface holding his plate. Brass pull-tabs trimmed the desk's middle drawers, and fancy carved handles decorated the roller top. "My Grandma Jacobs has something similar, but her desk is smaller. She was the tiny old lady at my parents' party in a bright yellow dress."

Alicia's gaze brightened. "I saw your grandma dancing with your dad. She might own a rolltop version of a secretary desk."

"I'll ask her the next time I visit."

"That's okay. I'll bet Kristi knows."

Damn it. His sister would. Away flew a handy excuse to check in with his grandma regarding her furniture choices and report back to Alicia.

"This desk belonged to my great-aunt," Alicia said in a soft voice. "Spats was her dog. And, well, she...my Great-Aunt Gert...passed away in December. It was unexpected. Even though she was eighty-eight, she was healthy and active."

"I'm sorry," Brady said. Losing someone Alicia loved would have churned up plenty of sadness. "It sounds like you and your aunt were close."

"We were." She chewed the inside of her cheek. "Gert was my mom's aunt. My mother died of breast cancer when I was four. My mom was sick for ages, but I was so little the memory feels like she disappeared on me one day. Like in a creepy fairy tale." She snapped her fingers. "Poof. Mommy's gone."

Brady's heart stumbled. "That's awful." The death of her mom sounded traumatic. And her Aunt Gert had died only seven months ago. Although, in his opinion, eighty-eight was a remarkable achievement.

These weren't crumbs, he realized. They were thick slices of Alicia Maxwell's life cake. Delivered in a hurry, as if she needed to convey the information as a bunch.

He touched her hand. "I want to say I know how you feel, but that sounds trite when I haven't been through it. One of my grandfathers has a pacemaker, but all four of my grandparents are alive."

"It's okay." Gaze lowering, she sipped her coffee. "I don't remember much about my mom, but I miss her anyway. There's a void,"—she put a hand over her heart—"in here."

He nodded, remaining silent, allowing her a moment to continue.

She drew in a breath. "After my mom died, Great-Aunt Gert stepped in so I wouldn't get totally swamped in testosterone. Which is a thing, in case you didn't know."

He allowed himself a smile. "I believe you."

"Gert wasn't around every day. My dad and my two oldest brothers raised me. The youngest two more or less put up with me." Alicia paused. "Gert was like a fun part-time grandma and friend. When my mom was young, Gert was this outspoken, bohemian figure in her life."

Brady hoisted his mug for another sip of coffee, wondering what she was getting at. "Gert sounds cool."

"She was," Alicia asserted. Appearing more at ease now that she was further into her story, she plucked a fluted chocolate off her frosted cupcake. "Gert never married." Alicia popped the chocolate into her mouth, chewed, and swallowed. "She didn't have kids. She was very independent."

"So are you. I admire that about you."

"I'm no pushover."

"No, ma'am."

She smiled. "Gert came from old family money. She traveled the world, indulged her whims, and donated time and cash to charity." She nodded toward her dog, who'd devoured his treat and trotted toward the desk. "Gert named Spats after her last lover."

Brady choked on a mouthful of hot coffee. "Excuse me?"

Alicia laughed. Her gaze assessed—and beguiled—him. She studied him as if she were testing his limits. Or was she challenging her own?

Her dog pawed her leg. She looked at the pooch. "No more treats for now, Mr. Spiff. Here, take Boo-Bear." She passed over the stuffed bear, and Spats scampered to his corner.

"Pietro Spatafora," she informed Brady, humor glinting in her eyes. "That was the guy's name." She ate a bite of cupcake.

"Your aunt's last lover?" Brady asked, and Alicia nodded. He peeled away his cupcake paper and savored the rich peanut-butter flavor, the chocolate on top, and a thick dollop of creamy frosting. "Is this Pietro fellow still alive?"

Nodding, she cleared crumbs from her fingertips. "As far as I know. He was an Italian pastry chef. Maybe he's retired now. He met my aunt during a temporary work visa while he was teaching a course at a Seattle culinary institute. My aunt and her best friend took a night school version of the class."

"They were his students?"

Alicia nodded again. "Gert was in her early seventies. Pietro was maybe sixty. It wasn't long before he and Gert began a dramatic love affair."

Okay. "Was she happy?"

"Not for long." Alicia's head tipped. "Pietro cheated on her. *With* her friend."

Brady frowned. "What kind of person does that?"

"In Pietro's case, it turned out he planned to, shall we say, sample every willing female student. Gert's bestie had a ton of excuses for why she risked a lifelong friendship for a few passionate nights with the man, but the betrayal hurt my aunt deeply. Pietro returned to Europe, and Gert threw herself into other pursuits...and other friends. A few years later, Gert got Spats from an animal rescue. She shortened the Spatafora surname for her new puppy."

"Why? Pietro was a jerk."

Alicia glanced away. "My great-aunt said she wanted a reminder that while love can bite you in the butt, taking the risk is worthwhile." She looked at him again. "Gert believed in finding the good in every experience. So when she died last winter following complications from a broken hip, she had no regrets."

Brady rubbed his chin. "Okay, I get it." He thought he did anyway. Her great-aunt had lived by a go-for-the-gusto philosophy. Regardless of how much Alicia had admired the woman, she hadn't reached the gusto stage of her life yet. Would she ever?

"Gert left me the funds to open Bitty Cakes. Then she donated the rest of her wealth to favorite charities."

"What about your brothers?"

"My dad and oldest brother knew about Gert's will for years. No one in my family had a problem with her wishes." Her gaze drifted to the ceiling. "How do I explain this?"

"Take your time."

Alicia glanced at him again. "My brothers have made smart investments and have rewarding careers. In our family, I'm the baby, and that's very much how my dad and brothers see me. It's frustrating. I didn't get time with our mom like they each did. She didn't hold my hand on my first day of school. My dad and brothers have looked out for me my whole life. Gert taking care of me in her will was like an extension of *them* taking care of me, if that makes sense."

"It does."

"I love my dad and brothers, but being the youngest in my family can feel smothering. At the same time, that they share similar careers leaves me feeling, I don't know, on the outskirts, I guess.

Growing up, I had no desire to force myself into the law-enforcement mold. It was as if I didn't quite fit." She pushed back a lock of her long, dark hair. "It's confusing."

"Not really." Every time they talked, Brady gained a clearer perspective on this fascinating woman. The more Alicia let him in, the more he wanted to creak open her gates. "You want to live your life in your own way. Like Gert."

Alicia beamed. "Yes! I must sound like a control beast—"

"You don't." Although she was more cryptic than his previous girlfriends. More interesting. And enthralling to the core.

"The irritating part is that I take longer than the average bear to decide what I want. I second-guess myself. I don't want to make a mistake."

Or experience more emotional pain, he suspected. "Mistakes are how we grow," he said, reaching across the few inches separating them. He held her hand. Her fingers trembled.

"I know," she replied, her gaze seeking his. "But I...I didn't expect you, Brady."

He glided his thumb over her middle knuckles. "I hope you mean that in the best possible way."

"I'm not sure how I mean it yet. Is that all right?"

Brows up, he nodded. "Yep."

She laughed, and her fingers slipped free of his grasp. "See, this is why you make me crazy. You're funny and sweet and considerate. You've only asked me out for coffee—a few times now—but it feels monumental. Like I'm on a reality TV dating show. Not only do I need to make a choice, but I need to make the *right* choice, or I'll turn around and you'll be gone. Forever."

Similar to the people she'd loved. He shook his head. "You're pressuring yourself. Alicia, I'm not going anywhere unless you tell me to. We're having coffee now, and it's not scary, is it?"

"No."

"Good. We're just two people sitting and talking. Getting to know each other. If having coffee is a step on a relationship list, we've slam-dunked this thing. It's out of the way."

Her lips pursed. "That confirms it. I'm incapable of agreeing to a simple coffee date. I *am* a freak of some sort."

He smiled. "Nah. You sound like someone who needs to move at her own pace."

"Okay, there. What you said?" She gestured at him. "Brady, you're understanding and patient. It makes me want to jump right in and kiss you."

He opened his hands. "I'm here."

He expected her to shake her head. Instead, she leaned forward in her chair. "Brady," she whispered, her fingertips swishing on the thighs of his uniform. "Please kiss me. And be quick about it, before I change my mind."

Heat rushed through his veins. "This isn't Truth or Dare."

"For me, it is. I'm daring myself. To a kiss."

"Even though I wear the uniform?"

"*While* you're wearing the uniform."

His chest tightened. He clasped her fingers again and rested their entangled hands on her lap.

Her lips brushed his, tasting of chocolate and peanut butter and creamy coffee. The kiss stayed gentle and romantic, their lips moving slowly and pleasurably. Undemanding.

As soon as the need to delve deeper licked his veins, he broke the kiss.

Their gazes locked, and her eyelashes fluttered.

"Wow," she whispered. "That was amazing." She touched her lips. "This could get complicated."

Brady nodded, heart thudding. Their fiery magnetism could kindle and glow. Or blister and burn.

Either way, he was up for finding out which way the fire would spin.

Chapter Six

The bubbly TV reporter held her microphone toward Alicia. "I'd say you have a hit on your hands!" The woman's toothy smile stretched across her face, reminding Alicia of a ventriloquist dummy in extreme chatterbox mode.

But who was she to judge? Adrenaline shot through her veins as she wrung her hands at the waist of her Capri pants. The thrill of appearing on live television amid curious customers milling in her shop vibrated to the soles of her serviceable workday sandals.

"Thank you," she spoke into the mic. She aimed a relaxed smile at the camera before slipping an appreciative glance to her dad and her two middle brothers, who'd stopped by for support. "I'm incredibly grateful to everyone who responded to the online coverage and has taken a chance on Bitty Cakes," she gushed, meaning every word. "My remarkable staff has been working nonstop." Both indoors and out on the sidewalk, Yuri and Kristi served samples of the July S'mores cupcake. Brady, dressed in civilian duds on this sunny Thursday morning, ran the cash register.

"Before we go," the reporter asked, "are there any new recipes coming for August? It's just around the corner."

"Yes." Alicia lowered her mouth to the mic again. "Our August special is a lovely Raspberry-Lemonade cupcake. Imagine enjoying refreshing pink lemonade during a picnic on a warm summer day. We'll have lemon-flavored bitty cakes with raspberry frosting, and fruit and citrus portions on top." She and Kristi had brainstormed serving the cakes in red-and-white-checkered paper cups evocative of 1950s picnic blankets.

"Sounds wonderful." The reporter's head swiveled back to the camera. "There you have it, folks. Come on down to Bitty Cakes for a taste of Rosevale cupcake heaven!" The woman's mega-smile remained glued in place until the camera operator signaled the end of the feed. The interviewer shook Alicia's hand. "Thank you very much."

"Thank you and your whole team. It's been a pleasure."

The reporter and her crew hustled out of the shop, carrying a complimentary box of cupcakes. Alicia took a moment to settle her nerves, smoothing her hands along her hips. Her life had changed rapidly in only five days, but especially in the two days since she and Brady kissed in her office.

But she refused to obsess about their kiss right now.

She glanced at her dad, who stood against the far wall with Ian and Aaron. Dad gave an affectionate nod. None of the Maxwell men had offered a word of advice since entering the shop. They were just *here*, which meant everything. Alicia's two other brothers had stayed away to reduce the effect of the Maxwell Testosterone Contingent. Had her family finally accepted her independence?

Then there was Brady...

She risked a glance toward the cash register. Brady responded with a wink, and her heart kicked into a rapid cadence. The man was here for more than her cupcakes, and he deserved a solid answer. He didn't have to keep showing up at her place of business, volunteering his time and tolerating her quirks. She wasn't forcing him to help, but she couldn't keep flip-flopping on him either.

She broke eye contact and wove through the crowd toward her family. She pecked Aaron and Ian on their cheeks before hugging their strong, tall father.

"Hi, Dad." A stream of love flowed through her. "Thanks for being here."

His arm curled around her shoulders. "I'm not missing my little girl's time in the spotlight."

A corner of Ian's mouth crooked up. "It's hard to believe you're stepping out on your own like this."

"Thanks," Alicia responded wryly. "Full of compliments, like always."

"Aw, I'm yanking your chain."

Alicia grinned. "Ditto."

Aaron, her other middle brother, knuckled her arm. "*I* knew you could do it." Aaron angled Ian a derisive glance.

Alicia rolled her eyes. Some things never changed, including the dynamics of large families. Her brothers hassled each other, but were friends as well as siblings, and they had each other's backs.

Dad motioned his head toward the other side of

the shop. Brady moved out from behind the till, providing his sister access to the cash drawer.

"Jacobs is keeping the Department happy, bringing in a box of your cupcakes each day," Dad said.

Aaron added, "I think Jacobs is trying to make a certain someone happy."

Alicia ignored Aaron's goading. "I can't believe my good luck, first with the positive reaction to the videos and then hiring someone as well-suited to the job as Kristi, thanks to Brady."

"Luck has nothing to do with it," Dad said. "Neither does Jacobs. Much. This is your win, Doodles." He used her childhood nickname.

Ian nodded. "Everything is falling in line, but you did the legwork. Great-Aunt Gert would be proud."

Alicia's insides softened. "Thanks, Ian."

"Bring it in," Dad said, and Alicia and her brothers joined hands-to-shoulders in a Maxwell family huddle.

She and Dad shared another hug as Ian's voice floated to her ears. "Aaron, are you grabbing that order we talked about?"

"You bet. I'm gonna chat up the cute clerk."

Alicia faced her brothers. "Which one? Yuri is married."

"That"—Aaron gestured across the room toward Kristi—"cute clerk with the big green eyes."

Brady reached their group. "Hey. That cute clerk is my sister."

Aaron's eyebrows arched. "Should I be worried?"

Ian patted Brady's shoulder. "Don't worry, Jacobs. I'll beat Aaron to a pulp if Kristi so much as frowns at him."

Alicia slipped Brady a glance. "He's mostly joking."

Good humor gleamed in Brady's eyes. He nodded at Ian. "Seems like you might beat up Aaron regardless."

Aaron scoffed and sauntered toward the till. "You know what they say about the best-laid plans," he drawled. "Any time on the attempt to strong-arm me, Ian," he tossed over his shoulder. "Name the place."

Alicia smiled at her siblings' antics. These two especially had roughhoused and boxed and wrestled for as long as she remembered. Brady didn't have brothers, but that didn't stop him from under-standing how to mesh with her crew. He was that great of a guy.

Brady engaged her dad in Briarton PD conversation fit for public consumption while Ian regaled her with funny anecdotes from his last two shifts with the Seattle City Police. Alicia half-listened. Too many thoughts crowded her mind. Right here, right now, these four were the men in her world—three Maxwells, plus Brady. If she added on her two absent brothers, the total amounted to *six* law-enforcement dudes.

Oh, boy. That was a lot.

She dragged in air. Even as an impressionable teenager dreaming about her future while brother after brother entered a police academy, following in their dad's footsteps, she'd sworn off ever having a cop boyfriend. The Maxwell men sometimes suffocated her with honorable intentions. Also, given her mom's untimely death, wasn't it enough that she fretted about losing another family member? Her dad or a brother? What rational woman invited those miseries into her romantic life? For Alicia, dating men in other occupations had been a logical solution. But that was before—

Her breath caught. Well, before Brady.

She hadn't anticipated a man like Brady Jacobs entering her life. Their kiss in her office two days ago had lit her up inside and out. Yes, she'd asked him to initiate the kiss, but now she wondered...was she rushing things with him to prove—if only to herself—that she wasn't a lava-hot mess?

Brady worked with her father. And his sister worked for *her*—for Alicia.

And she felt great about Kristi, who seemed destined to become her assistant for real.

If Kristi worked out for Bitty Cakes, what would happen if Alicia and Brady didn't go the distance? Would Alicia experience another unwanted emotional upheaval?

Ian's voice broke into her musings. "She's in Doodlesville." Ian prodded her shoulder. "Alicia? You off gallivanting with your buddy, Doodles?"

She shook her head. "It's nothing to do with Doodles." She directed her gaze to Aaron, who returned with two boxes of Bitty Cakes.

Aaron chuckled. "She was off with Doodles."

Alicia's jaw tensed. "I *wasn't* with Doodles." They were treating her like a child again.

Brady's eyebrows lifted. "Who's Doodles?"

Her brothers laughed.

"Knock it off," Dad said, steering his sons toward the exit. As Ian reached the bakery door, Aaron flipped open the Bitty Cakes box and destroyed half a cupcake in one bite.

Brady smiled at Alicia. "So? This Doodles?"

She exhaled. "Doodles was my pretend poodle when I was little. Other kids have imaginary playmates. I had an imaginary dog."

"Your family didn't have a dog?" Brady asked in a tone implying she'd missed out. "We had a rescue Pittie named Mutt, two cats from the same mama, and a turtle."

That sounded almost overwhelming. "We had a retired K9 German Shepherd named Ranger. He was more the boys' dog, so I created Doodles." She paused. "I want to make it clear I wasn't thinking about an imaginary pet just now. I have Spats. There's no need for Doodles."

A glint entered Brady's eyes. "What *were* you thinking about?"

She shifted her gaze to an invisible point above his left shoulder. "Stuff."

"Oh? Such as?"

She focused on a spot beside his right biceps. "Um, stuff about me and—"

"Me?" he interrupted." I hope so. Stuff about you and me?"

She considered denying the truth, but what was the use? He saw straight through her.

She looked at him. "Yes."

"In case it makes it easier on you, I don't have time for coffee today. That'll give you more thinking time."

She groaned. She was so obvious. "Thanks."

"Now, about Saturday night. I'm not working. Can I drop by your place? We can talk about what happened in your office."

He must mean their kiss. Her lips buzzed as if he'd kissed her again, amid the bustling throng of Bitty Cakes customers.

"I don't know," she answered honestly.

"It's not a date," he said. "If you want, invite a friend. In fact, I can bring a friend to meet *your* friend, if a group situation feels more comfortable."

"Most of my friends have boyfriends." Or a fiancé, in Tania's case.

He shrugged. "As long as we have time to talk, I'm down for the two of us or a group sitch. Remember, it's not a date."

"Not a date," Alicia repeated. "Agreed." But what if she got the urge to jump his bones? And *not* in a group sitch? Would getting frisky with Brady make it a date?

"Great. I'm only a guy showing up at your apartment. Not expecting cupcakes. Or anything else." A low huskiness reverberated in his voice. "I'm just looking to discuss...and possibly discover..."

Oh, God. His words radiated raw desire. She ached to kiss him again. Deeply. Intimately.

She craved his touch. On her lips. On her body.

But was her heart ready to *discover*?

Chapter Seven

Alicia walked around the dinette table in her cozy apartment, pouring cups of tea for herself, Lacey, and her good friend, Claire. Spats snored on a T-shirt at the base of a chair while Claire spoiled the pooch with a bare-footed belly rub.

Alicia placed the teapot on a trivet and sat opposite Lacey. Both friends slipped her curious glances.

"All right," she said, sensing she was about to receive some caring flak. "Let me have it." She picked up her mug.

Lacey's head tipped. "Can I just say this isn't how I pictured my Saturday night playing out." It wasn't a question.

Alicia winced. "I know, and I'm sorry. Brady said to invite my friends." She couldn't stop a smile from twitching on her lips as she recalled his words in the bakery on Thursday: *"I'm looking to discuss...and possibly discover."* A sensuous shiver whispered through her. She sipped her tea to distract herself from the memory, savoring the cinnamon-spice flavor. Aromatic steam curled from the mug, and the ceramic surface warmed her lips.

Claire said, "If I remember the story correctly, Brady said if you invited a friend then he would too. But he isn't bringing anyone to meet either of us, right? We're happily off the market."

"Happily," Lacey stressed from over her mug.

Alicia waved a hand. "Those are pesky details. I need emotional support. You two are it." She liked Brady. *So* much. It wouldn't take much more exposure to the man to visualize them together long into the future. Her pulse raced. The thought of accepting her growing feelings scared her. Never mind her rule about not dating cops. It wasn't like her to get swept off her feet. Yet here she teetered on the edge of a speedy fall.

"I can't string him along while I bounce back and forth," she informed her friends. A steadfast man like Brady Jacobs deserved a woman willing to put her heart on the line, not someone with the toes of one foot dipping into a tempting pond while the other remained firmly planted on the grass-covered bank.

Lacey's expression softened. "Aw, Alicia. You seem to like Brady an awful lot, and he's plainly into you. What's holding you back?"

Alicia glanced into her tea. "Everything is coming at me at a breakneck pace, and I don't know if I can keep up." She curled a hand in front of her chest. "The changes at work, the last-minute preparations for Tania and Trey's wedding, and—and the feelings I get whenever Brady is within spitting distance." Or kissing distance. A humming sensation danced along her lips. "It's like I'm spinning on a merry-go-round. Not a fancy carousel with painted horses and merry music, but one of those deathtraps we played on in the park as kids. What if I fly off and bang my head? I might get a concussion." Honest to God, that was how she felt.

Claire and Lacey exchanged sympathetic glances.

"You're taking the playground analogy too far," Claire said, her concerned gaze resting on Alicia. "When you first met Brady at your dad's work barbecue, did you experience these same off-kilter sensations?"

Alicia nodded. "It sounds illogical. Is it normal?"

Lacey snorted. "Yep." She grinned.

Claire continued, "You've taken a chance on other guys, had good relationships and fun sexy times. Why not throw the dice with Brady?"

"I don't want to hurt him." What if her powerful feelings didn't last? "Aside from some dates with Derek—which Janie talked us into, I might add— I've seriously avoided men in blue. Not family members or friends, of course, but in relationships." She looked at Lacey. "You and I discussed this. I grew up in the life. There's a ton of sacrifice, and I decided years ago, no way, it's not for me. If I ignored those warning bells to start something with Brady, what if it doesn't work out and I break his heart? Or wonder if we split up in a few months and things become awkward with his sister? I have a good feeling about Kristi and Bitty Cakes. I really do."

"And you *don't* have a good feeling about Brady?" Lacey prodded, poking holes in Alicia's thought processes.

"Well..." Not that she wanted to admit.

Lacey's eyebrows arched. "Want my opinion?"

Alicia held her breath. "Sure."

Her friend twirled a finger. "Your concerns about Kristi are a smokescreen. You're afraid of *getting* hurt as much as you're worried about hurting your handsome cop."

Claire nodded. "Lacey has a point. Alicia, what's the alternative? You'll let Brady walk away to find love with someone else? If you don't dig beneath his badge to see him for the awesome human being he is, you might miss out on something amazing."

"But—" Was she brave enough to confess the root of the problem to her friends? That she didn't envision staying with Brady for six months or a year, longer time frames than previous relationships. She pictured falling *in love* with the man. Within the next week. Or maybe tomorrow.

Or tonight when she saw him again!

Panic fluttered beneath her breastbone. She, Alicia Maxwell, took baby steps, not leaps off a cliff. She perambulated. She didn't sky dive.

What if she allowed her feelings for Brady to develop, only to lose him to the dangers of his job? Her dad and brothers hadn't been hurt on the streets, but that didn't mean Brady would enjoy an incident-free career. In police work, anything could happen. To any of the men she loved. At any time!

"Sudden romances are fun," Lacey said. "Claire and I are now experts. I mean, who knows what will happen with me and Derek? He could hurt me. I could hurt him. Right now, I predict sunshine and daisies, but let's be realistic. We're eight days in."

Claire nodded. "And Ridge and I have been together a week. But I can tell you sure as I'm sitting here, no matter what comes down the line, I will never—and I mean *never*—regret running out of Tania's bridesmaid dress fitting to hop onto Ridge's motorcycle."

Lacey glanced at Claire. "And you zoomed away with your man while wearing your maid-of-honor duds. That's next-level romantic." Her eyes glimmered. "Janie filled me in on the salon disaster."

Claire groaned. "That ugly coral dress is toast. Ridge and I made sure of it." Claire preened on her chair. "The next day, Tania and I worked magic on the purple gown. *It* is perfect. So is Ridge. And his ridge is perfect." She wiggled her eyebrows, and Alicia and her friends chuckled.

"Braggart," Alicia said, glad the focus had shifted off her.

"I love the girl talk," Lacey responded. "By the way, Derek and I *celebrated*,"—she sing-songed—"Thursday night after my meeting with Clemmons Consulting."

Alicia beamed. "I'm glad Clemmons gave you an offer."

"My bosses are clever cookies," Claire remarked.

"I'll say," Lacey agreed. She studied Alicia, then tapped the table. "Here's an idea about Brady. Ask yourself, what would Great-Aunt Gert do?"

Alicia shrugged. "That's simple. She would take the plunge."

Claire and Lacey swapped another look.

"Sounds smart." This from Lacey.

"A no-brainer." That from Claire.

"Yeah, yeah." Alicia wouldn't repeat the now-legendary tale amongst her friend group about how her great-aunt had embarked on her first skiing lesson at eighty-eight, flirted with the instructor, skidded out of control on the bunny hill, and ultimately sustained a life-ending injury. After discussing the Brady situation, it had become clear as cut glass that she needed to reach her own conclusions. Not base her choices on Gert's philosophy, even though she'd promised her relative she would explore her adventurous side. If she located it.

Neither should she rule against Brady because he was a police officer. She was twenty-six, not sixteen. She could change her mind.

A knock rapped at the door, and her pulse zip-zapped in her veins.

"Girl talk is over," Lacey announced with a wink across the table. "Rev your engines, Alicia. It's guy time."

In the hall outside Alicia's apartment, Brady pasted on an amiable smile, stomach knotting. Tonight, one way or another, they would sort out the nature of their relationship. If Alicia wasn't into dating *him* specifically, he would beat a retreat to the friend zone—the last place he wanted to be. But he would suck it up. For Alicia's sake and for his sister's. He didn't have another choice.

The door opened, and Alicia peeked around the jamb. "Hi," she murmured.

A heavy warmth stirred in his chest. "I brought wine." He hefted a bottle of smoky Walla Walla Valley Syrah.

A female voice sailed from inside. "Thanks, but we're having tea."

Alicia blushed. "Come in."

Brady grinned. "I did say to invite a friend." He stepped into the small living room. Two women sat at the dinette table, one a smiling brunette, and he recognized the blonde and her voice from earlier this week—Lacey, the lingerie designer. "Hello." He waved at the pair. "I'm Brady."

Lacey waved back. "We've heard. I'm Lacey."

"I've heard," he responded, sliding Alicia a glance. Man, he longed to kiss her again. A pale pink skirt shaped her hips, and a scooped-neck T-shirt hugged her curves like the tastiest cupcake frosting on earth. But a deeper sentiment bubbled beneath his physical cravings. One he hadn't experienced with another woman, and it was wholly tender and genuine. He wanted to stroll arm-in-arm into this new emotional landscape with Alicia.

He offered another smile, which she reciprocated.

"This is Claire," Alicia introduced the brunette with wavy brown hair as she and Brady walked to the table.

"Hey," he greeted.

"Hey," Claire parroted, fingers wiggling.

Brady darted a look at Spats. The dog stretched beneath the table and woofed. "Hi, boy." Brady handed Alicia the wine. "Save this for another time. Tea sounds great." He had no clue—he was a black coffee guy—but he wanted to fit in with her group.

"Thank you. How thoughtful." Studying the

label, she headed for the kitchen tucked into a recessed nook.

Brady sat in the empty chair to Lacey's left and accepted a mug of tea when Alicia returned. Alicia took the seat to his right.

Lacey gestured at herself and Claire. "Our guys are working tonight," Lacey said.

Brady nodded. "How do you three ladies know each other?" He drank a mouthful of cinnamon-flavored tea. Kind of weak for a caffeine infusion but tolerable.

Lacey gestured toward the entryway. "I live across the hall. Alicia and I met in the neighborhood a few times when she lived in another building in the complex. She needed to change apartments to keep Spats, and now we're super close."

"We sure are," Alicia said. "Claire and I met in ninth grade. She and I are both bridesmaids for Tania's wedding."

"The wedding that's happening next weekend?" Brady asked.

"Yes," Alicia responded. She and her friends clinked mugs, and he followed suit.

Lacey double-tapped his mug. "We're a tight group but open to more members." A mischievous smile curved her lips. "Isn't that right, Claire?"

"Always." Claire's gaze flitted from Brady to Alicia. A second later, she typed a text on her phone. "I thought of something," she said to Lacey, scratching her cheek. "When the groomsmen from out of town arrive—" Her phone vibrated, and she scanned a message. Her eyes widened. "Oh, no!" She tapped a reply. "The bride is having a teensy meltdown."

Brady suppressed a chuckle at her dramatic tone.

Alicia's forehead creased. "What's wrong?"

"Just some tweaking of wedding-night apparel," Claire replied, standing up. "Nothing requiring your input. Lacey, can we convene in the kitchen?" She wrinkled her nose at Brady. "Girl stuff. Totally Boring."

Lacey trotted after Claire. *"Boring? I* designed Tania's negligee. It's dreamy and romantic and tear-it-off-me-right-this-minute. What's her problem?"

Brady fastened his gaze on Alicia's blue watchful one. "I like your friends." While Claire and Lacey wouldn't win acting awards, it seemed he'd found allies within Alicia's circle. But what he really wanted was to connect with *her.*

She bit a thumbnail. "It's weird I invited them, isn't it?" she asked in a soft voice.

He smiled. "I suggested it."

"True. Which somehow makes me feel weirder for doing it." She inhaled. "Brady, you're the most understanding guy I know met, but—"

A stone of dread dropped in his stomach. There it was. The infamous B word: *But*. No guy as overwhelmingly drawn as he was to Alicia wanted to hear the B word.

"Hey." Leaning forward, he clasped her hand. "Do you need to tell me something?" Like that the B word was doomed to spiral him closer to the hated F phrase. As in Friend Zone.

Her fingers curled in his. "This isn't the time," she said, glancing over her shoulder at her friends. The pair stood at the kitchen counter, arms folded across their middles and their heads bowed. The barely discernible thread of their conversation focused on wedding details.

Alicia gazed at him again. "You'll think I'm silly."

"Try me," he whispered, holding her hand and stroking her wrist. The light scent of her summery perfume drifted to his nostrils. Her friends faded away from his peripheral vision. In this moment, Alicia was his world.

She leaned closer, and her long hair spilled over one shoulder. "This is difficult for me to explain," she whispered. "I've lost people I love. My mom. My great-aunt. I'm…afraid of losing somebody else." Color flared on her cheeks.

"You mean like if something happened to your dad or a brother? That makes sense." Brady swallowed a curse. He was a colossal lunkhead. The risks in her family's professions were obvious. It didn't matter if her brothers and father had—so far—emerged unscathed. Sitting around the dinner table growing up, she would have heard so many frightening stories and near-misses. Then *he* came along, wanting something she might not feel prepared to offer.

She nodded. "I look ahead too much. You could say I fixate. It's just that, well, if I really like a guy, and if he's a cop—"

"I get it," Brady responded in a calm voice, although an excited part of him realized that in a roundabout way she'd admitted she liked *him*. More than she'd expected?

Her gaze cut to his. "It doesn't help that my cousin's new husband got shot a couple of years ago," she whispered. "On the job."

"Oh, boy." Brady paused, absorbing this new information. "That's rough." The cards had once more stacked against him. "The husband is—was—

a cop?" he surmised, arrowing a glance toward the kitchen. Alicia's friends chatted while tidying the counter and emptying the dish rack. Claire opened the fridge. The women's heads ducked behind the appliance door.

Alicia's eyes misted. "It happened in Portland. Only two weeks after their honeymoon."

Elbows on his knees, Brady leaned closer. "Tell me what happened." He hoped she felt comfortable enough to address her fears. He yearned for her to feel safe.

"Darren wound up okay," she went on in quiet tones. "He was wounded in the hand. But it could have been far worse. One day, he and Kaylee—my cousin—were newlyweds. Happy, giddy, making plans. Then life swept in like a rogue wave and whacked them sideways." She flicked a glance toward her friends. "Claire and Lacey don't know the details. My family knows Darren got injured and that he recovered, but they don't realize how deeply the experience affected Kaylee. She was my best friend growing up, and she needed someone to confide in." Alicia breathed in.

"That someone was you," Brady concluded. His compassionate Alicia carried the weight of more than her fair share of loss.

She gave a tremulous smile. "Kaylee and I called or texted every day for a month." She wet her lips. "Darren got trapped in a scary hostage situation. It was a domestic violence incident that spiraled out of control. Police were hiding behind vehicles trying to storm the house while Darren did his best to talk the guy down. The guy went wild, swinging his gun. That's when Darren got shot. Kaylee had horrible nightmares for weeks, imagining the worst. Helping her through the ordeal made me have some nightmares too. About my dad and brothers. About when I lost my mom." Her gaze lowered to her lap.

"Hey," Brady soothed, clasping her hands. "It's normal to feel scared about those things."

"I know, but I can't pretend they didn't affect me." She drew in another long breath. "Kaylee went to counseling and seems fine, but her troubles reminded me how quickly life can change. As a teenager, I vowed never to marry a cop. Or to even taking a step toward the possibility. What happened to my cousin when she and her husband were first married sort of solidified my feelings on the subject."

Brady puffed out a slow stream of air. They were heading down a road that seemed destined to end at a fifty-foot-tall stop sign. "From what you've said,

I'm guessing even at the dating stage you'd prefer a guy who doesn't climb into a uniform that symbolizes putting his life on the line every day."

"Yes." She chewed her bottom lip. "I told you it was silly."

"It's not. Your feelings are justified." He rubbed the fleshy part of her hand between her thumb and forefinger. The fridge door thumped as it closed in the kitchen. Out of the corner of an eye, he spied Claire and Lacey returning. Each woman carried two bowls of ice cream. "Alicia, it's okay," he whispered as her friends approached. "I understand. We can be friends."

"I don't want that either. I want—" She gave a frustrated and adorable growl. "Brady, In a perfect world, I'd snap my fingers and make my stumbling blocks disappear."

He tried a supportive smile. "Don't lose hope. You can. *We* can. Together."

"You're sweet." Her eyes glistened, but she smiled back. "I need a minute." She bounced off her chair without glancing around—and crashed into Lacey. One ice cream bowl tumbled against Lacey's chest, smearing the underwear designer's top with a streak of vanilla. The spoons clanked to the floor.

Alicia's eyes popped. "I'm sorry!" She looked at Brady. "I'm not normally a klutz."

He lifted his hands. "It's okay." The similarities between the chaos at his parents' anniversary party and tonight's ice cream tumble weren't lost on him. If he escaped the friend zone with Alicia, the events would make a cute future how-we-met story. His chest warmed.

Lacey rescued the bowls and plunked them on the table. Spats popped up and slurped frosty lumps off the floor. Brady fetched the spoons as Alicia disappeared into the bathroom with Lacey.

"She *isn't* normally a klutz," Claire told him.

"A calamity now and then doesn't worry me." But did it worry Alicia?

Claire put her bowls on the table. "I'll get a cloth. And clean spoons." She hurried to the kitchen.

Brady accepted the cloth when Claire returned. Crouching, he scrubbed the mess while she rearranged place settings.

Spats stared at the lack of ice cream on the floor and whined.

Brady *felt* like whining.

"Dog, I am doomed," he mumbled.

Chapter Eight

Alicia spun in a circle in her tiny bathroom, raking her fingers through her hair. "Gah, I've done it now," she said to Lacey, face flaming as if she'd swallowed a flask of Louisiana pepper sauce. "Knocking ice cream all over you and freaking out over something that might not ever happen." Worrying over losing Brady to the dangers of his job, when, technically, he wasn't *hers* yet. At this rate, he might never be. "Brady must think I've gone over the line."

Lacey wiped ice cream off her top with a damp facecloth. "Alicia, what's going on? What did he say? Was he an ass? If that's the case, I'll take him down. Just say the word." Lacey tossed the cloth into the sink and crooked a tough-chick elbow.

Alicia snatched a tissue from the box on the vanity and honked her nose. "It's not him. It's me."

"*You?*" Lacey snorted. "How can it be you? You're wonderful."

"I'm bonkers."

"You know what?" Lacey crossed her arms. "There's nothing wrong with that. Into each life a little bongo must fall. So my mom says."

Alicia's lips wobbled into an approximation of a smile. "There's something you don't know." She crumpled the tissue into the trashcan. At the sink, she washed and dried her hands.

"Is it something to do with Tania's wedding?" Lacey asked.

"No. It *should* be about wedding stress." Alicia faced her friend. "This summer was supposed to be about Tania and Trey, not me and my hangups." She thumped a fist on her chest. Until she'd unloaded on Brady tonight, she hadn't realized how much emotion she'd bottled up for years.

Over the last several months, she'd embarked on an ill-conceived and not-altogether-deliberate plan to avoid every facet of her life that didn't revolve around wedding activities or promoting Bitty Cakes. Her avoidance strategy had included shirking her feelings for Brady, who was the sweetest—and the hottest—guy she'd ever met. She couldn't switch off the lightbulb glaring the truth. She'd buried fears stemming from her mom's death deeper than a doomsday-prepper's bunker.

She opened her hands. "I thought I had my future planned out. My business, the type of man I looked forward to bringing into my life. I was one hundred percent positive I could never in a million years fall for a cop."

Lacey's lips pursed. "But then you met Brady?"

Alicia nodded. "Our attraction knocked me on my butt."

"Sounds incredible."

"Then why have I made it extra-complicated?" Massaging the base of her skull, Alicia paced the small bathroom. She strode from the sink to the tub, expressing the black hole of helplessness she'd experienced at a far too young age after her mom died. Described her cousin Kaylee's struggles and how Darren's shooting triggered nightmares in not only Kaylee but also in Alicia. "Focusing on Bitty Cakes helped me block out everything else. But running myself ragged wasn't the answer."

Lacey pressed her palms together yoga-style. "Alicia, Claire and I are feeling the pressure of our lives changing at hurricane-speed, but it doesn't compare to what you've gone through. Honey, I'm so sorry you felt like you needed to keep your stressors to yourself." She enveloped Alicia in a tight hug.

"Well, you know what they say." Alicia sniffled against her friend's shoulder. "That was my bone-headed choice."

"It's quite the opposite. You care."

Alicia stepped out of Lacey's arms, heart melting. She had the most supportive friends. Could she expand her circle to include an amazing boyfriend?

A rap sounded at the door. "Hey, you two," Claire whispered, coming in and closing the door. "You've been in here ten minutes. Brady and I are hitting it off, but every time we catch a snippet of one of your voices, his ears perk up like a Doberman Pinscher's." She looked at Alicia. "He seems super tuned in to your voice in particular."

Alicia blew out a breath. "See?" she whispered. "This is another reason I have a rule against dating cops. They're super tuned in to *everything*."

Claire's eyes sparkled. "Imagine that kind of attention in the bedroom."

Alicia sighed. "I have."

"This is cute," Lacey said with a smile. "I'm dating a cop." She pointed at Claire. "You're dating a medical student who strips as a cop." Her finger swung toward Alicia. "And if you play your cards right, you'll be dating a cop."

Alicia groaned. "It's a cop infestation in our lives."

Claire put a finger to her chin. "I missed a step in the conversation, but I want to add my two cents." She ran her hands up Alicia's arms. "Sweetie, if Brady was a dud, your dad or one of your brothers would have said something about a thousand years ago. The Maxwell Testosterone Contingent is on your side. You're lucky to have them, even if they get on your nerves."

Lacey nodded. "Brady is a big boy. If he gets hurt, he'll deal with it. If you get hurt, we're here to pull you through. *Always.*"

Happiness built inside Alicia. "You're both right. Thank you." Their girlfriend group was incredible, but this pair especially had her back. So did her dad and brothers. No matter the challenges she faced in life, she couldn't go wrong. Love and encouragement were hers whenever she needed.

Claire touched her hand. "What's the verdict? Does Brady stay or go?"

She released a breath. "I need to catch you up on a few things. Tomorrow or the next day. It depends on what happens tonight with Brady."

"Ooh." Claire's eyebrows lifted. "I like where this is headed."

"Where *is* this headed?" Lacey asked.

Alicia's heart raced. "The details are for Brady alone. But I'm not letting him leave until I boot him out of the friend zone." She glanced at her messy-haired reflection in the mirror. "First, a makeup intervention."

Lacey plucked a brush from a holder on the vanity. "Don't forget your rat's nest."

Hands in his front jeans' pockets, Brady gazed down at Alicia's dog. For the umpteenth time, Spats pawed his leg. "*Now*, buddy?" Brady asked. "You need to go outside this very minute?"

Spats whimpered.

"I'll take that as a yes." Brady had eliminated any other possible conclusion. After Claire had vanished into the mysterious abyss of the female bathroom group meeting, he'd fed Spats a dog biscuit in the kitchen, but the snack hadn't settled the animal. He'd entertained the dog with a toy. Not even Boo-Bear interested the finicky canine.

"The women are busy," he told the animal. He

looked at the bathroom door. Were his chances with Alicia so dismal that she required an advisory panel before deciding how to proceed?

Spats trundled to the apartment's entryway and whined.

Yep, the dog needed to go out. Brady wasn't keen on interrupting Alicia's relationship summit, but he couldn't in all conscience remove Spats from the premises without her consent. He wouldn't stay here, period, if she didn't want him.

"All right," he said to Spats. Dog at his heels, he strode to the bathroom and knocked. "Are you ladies decent?"

Lacey's voice carried through the panel. "We're decently disturbed."

"We're decent," Alicia's voice followed.

A pang pierced Brady's heart as he recalled her story about her cousin. He was a softie for Ms. Alicia Maxwell, even if she handed him a one-way ticket to the friend zone. He just needed her in his life. If that was as his sister's boss, he'd buy the hell out of her cupcakes.

He leaned against the door. "Alicia, unless I'm misinterpreting your dog's signals, Spats needs a walk."

The bathroom door opened, and Brady gazed

into the room. At his feet, the dachshund's nose poked between his shins. They both stared at Alicia standing with a hip against the vanity, her gaze less doomsday than when she'd ducked inside. Brady's spirits lifted.

"Looks crowded in here," he said with a smile, noting Claire perched on the edge of the tub. Lacey sat on the lowered toilet lid. As if expecting instructions, the two women gazed at Alicia.

"It's jam-packed," she agreed.

Was that his cue to leave? He focused on her. "If tonight isn't a good time for us to talk, I can go. I'll walk Spats first if you and your friends need space. The living room couch looks more comfortable than the toilet and the tub. Just saying."

Alicia shook her head. "I want you to stay, Brady. Please." She stepped away from the vanity, revealing various cosmetics scattered around the sink. "Claire and Lacey can walk Spats. Right, girls?" She looked at her friends.

The women nodded.

Brady's heart thumped in his ears. Did he stand a solid chance with her?

"One more minute," she said, smile nervous. "I need to settle something."

The door shut in his face.

Chapter Nine

Alicia ushered her friends out of the apartment, Lacey in charge of Spats in a harness. The dog lunged into the corridor.

Alicia whispered to Claire, "Walk Spats for an hour, okay?"

"No problem." Claire tucked doggy bags and treats into a pocket.

"Thanks. And, Lacey?"

"Yeah?"

"After the walk, can he nap at your place for another hour?"

"Sure thing." Lacey restrained the dog with a twist of the leash handle. "Text if you need the little guy to sleep overnight. Derek is coming by after his shift, but he likes Spats. We'll spoil your dog rotten."

Alicia smiled. "Thank you for the offer. I'll see how it goes." She risked a glance over her shoulder. Brady sat on the living room sofa, his back to the entryway, affording her privacy with her friends and waiting for her.

She telepathed a silent message: *Thank you for waiting*.

The man possessed the patience of a monk. She intended to reward him. How would he react to her change of heart?

She looked at her friends and whispered, "If I regret what happens with Brady tonight, so what? You two are right. Great-Aunt Gert was right. Life is short. Life is for living in the moment."

"*And* for the future," Claire commented.

"Life is for living right to the end," Lacey said, corralling Spats at her feet. "Have fun."

"I will," Alicia responded, closing the door behind her friends and pooch. Sexy fun was the idea. But she wouldn't blame Brady if he'd hit enough roadblocks and didn't want to spend another moment in her wishy-washy company.

Well, she'd decided. Enough with the washy. She yearned for the wishy. As in a wish, a plan, a fiery desire that tonight exploded with passion and more intimate talks. That Brady felt as in tune to her as she felt with him.

Because she was *finally* moving forward. Releasing the shadows of her past and devoting herself not only to her business but also to her love life. She wanted to reach eighty-eight years old with zero regrets in the heart department.

Brady glanced around as the door clicked shut. "It's settled? We're talking?"

If things went her way, they were doing more than talking. Nodding, she motioned him to stay on the couch. She glided her palms along her skirt as she walked to the striped sofa and sat beside him. Her right knee grazed his denim-covered leg.

"I'm sorry for putting you through this," she murmured.

His green eyes twinkled—one of his sexiest superpowers. "It's not an issue." He clasped her hand and brushed a finger along her jaw, leaving a trail of shivery sensations on her neck. "Except for when you closed the bathroom door in my face," he stated, expression traffic-stop-cop serious. "That was—"

"Rude." Alicia cringed. "I'm sorry."

"It's okay." He ran two fingers of his free hand from her temple to where her hair glided over her shoulder. More shivery sensations radiated over her collarbone—and lower. Into her abdomen. Into her hips and core.

"You have plenty of reasons to stay clear of me," he said, the husky timbre of his deep voice relaying heartfelt understanding. "Losing your mom and suffering those bad dreams as a child. About *her*, but also about your dad and brothers. Living with every one of your brothers choosing to become a police officer, along with the uncertainty that entails. Going through tough days during your cousin's trauma. I get it." He whispered, "Alicia, who am I to impose a timetable on you?"

Her insides heated. Brady was so good to her. He was good *for* her. He helped her believe in possibilities. If she eased up and allowed life to unfurl instead of fighting it every damn second, decades of happiness lay within reach.

"Oh, I don't know," she said lightly. "I'd say you're a guy who'd like an answer." She interlocked their fingers on her lap. The warmth of his touch toasted her skin.

He smiled. "True." He looked at their hands. Thumb caressing her knuckles, he glanced up. "But—and this is important, sweetheart, so listen close-ly." He gazed into her eyes, and tenderness blossomed in her heart. "Phone me when you're ready. I could pretend I'll find someone else, but the truth is you've got me, Alicia. I'm hooked. Part of me realized the seriousness of my feelings when we first met in your dad's backyard. After getting to know you on a deeper level, the feelings have grown stronger. When you confided in me tonight, I was done." He winked. "In a good way done."

Tears of happiness pricked her eyes. "I thought my waffling might scare you off."

He shook his head. "I am *hooked*. I don't mind waiting. I thought I wanted an answer tonight. But while you and your friends were in the bathroom, I thought over our private conversations. If I'd had tough family times when I was young, I might be cautious too. Instead, I'm patient."

He paused, and her heart pounded.

"I have to say *I'm* not patient at this point," she said, and he chuckled.

"Alicia, I can wait as long as you need. It might drive me wild because I want you with the intensity of five thousand burning suns, but I can do it. If you ever want me to *stop* waiting—and by that, I mean take my lumps and be on my way—tell me. In person, a phone call, or a text. Just don't pull a ghost routine and disappear. Let me know."

Alicia's lips trembled. How had she gotten so lucky? To run into Brady time and again until she'd woken up to the prospect of forever?

"I don't want you to wait," she whispered, heart beating. "I don't want either of us to wait another moment. Brady..." She breathed out his name on a dreamy sigh. As she relaxed against his heat and solid muscle, she savored a blissful moment of anticipation before kissing him.

His warm lips invited her to sink into his strength. To discover the magical mysteries of honesty, trust, and vibrant emotion. She slid a hand behind his neck and rested her forehead on his.

"The idea of being with you freaked me out," she admitted in a quiet voice. "But not anymore."

He brushed a fingertip along her lips. "Was I too intense?"

"No." Her hand drifted off his neck. "You were determined, which was what I needed. Brady, we have something special, and I...wasn't ready. I didn't know how to deal with my feelings. They're here, they're strong, and they're not going anywhere." She played with his shirt buttons.

Gaze steady, he tipped up her chin. "Does it help you to know I feel the same?"

Her breath caught in her throat. "You do?"

He placed a tender kiss on her mouth. "I do."

Alicia's heart swelled. In one week, Tania and Trey would speak those words in a church with family and loved ones supporting them. Alicia believed that one day she and Brady would exchange vows. Because she didn't sense 'for now' with this man. She sensed a future of happiness and challenges and triumphs.

"Then let's take that chance together," she whispered, stepping onto the biggest metaphorical limb on the tallest imaginary tree of her life. Unbuttoning his shirt, she said, "I want to take that chance with you right now." She flattened her palms on the sturdy planes of his chest, relishing the dusting of crisp dark hair beneath her fingers.

Brady moaned. "*Alicia.*"

She kissed him as the pleasurable weight of his hands skated over her shoulders. His touch ran along her cotton top and settled on her hips below her short skirt. His hand slipped beneath the garment and cupped her bottom over her silky panties. Alicia's arousal flourished as his other hand played with the scooped neckline of her T-shirt before inching toward her bra strap, his fingertips rough and gentle. The perfect combination.

She rubbed his erection through his jeans. His

hips pushed forward. She whispered, "I'll get a condom."

He blinked. "Yeah?"

"Yeah." She kissed him. "Stay here." She drew in a breath. "Lacey offered to keep Spats at her place overnight. There's a bag of dog food and a couple of his toys there." Heart in her throat, she asked, "Do you have an opinion on my dog's plans for the evening?"

"*Hell, yeah*. I approve."

Alicia grinned. "I'll confirm with Lacey." She picked up her phone and sent a text. Wriggling her shoulders and giving Brady a flirtatious glance, she disappeared into her bedroom.

Minutes later, she opened the door, holding a condom packet and wearing nothing but her birthday suit. She slid an arm up the doorjamb and cocked her opposite hip. Sensation zinged to her center. She had leaped off a cliff, and her heart cascaded like a thunderous waterfall in her chest. Did Brady like what he saw?

His heated gaze devoured her woman parts. "Alicia," he said hoarsely, standing. "You surprised me. Honey, you're gorgeous."

Her nipples tingled and tightened. "Someone is

wearing too many clothes," she whispered, curling a finger toward her handsome man.

"That's easy to rectify." He ripped off his shirt and undressed faster than a comic-book hero. Except he *looked* as if he'd stepped out of the pages of a romance novel. Glorious butt, muscular chest, strong thighs, and a thick erection.

She was a lucky woman.

He left a pile of clothes on her living room floor and stepped forward.

"This way," she half-whispered, bringing out her sassy side as she handed him the condom and strolled to her bed, hips swaying. "This first time, I'm gonna need it hard and fast," she said, sensual hunger growing.

She was so ready for him. For Brady. It had been so long since she'd shared her body, and he was the only man she'd fantasized about in ten months. Since they'd met.

"Yes, ma'am," he replied in a gruff and utterly seductive voice that turned her on even more.

She'd rearranged the bedcovers while getting naked, and Brady set the condom packet on the night table before slipping beneath the sheets, reaching for her and tugging her close, his mouth on hers, tongue delving. She met him kiss for kiss, her hands running over his abs, her fingers grazing his stiff length. She curled her hand around his arousal and stroked, eliciting a groan from deep inside his chest.

He brushed a finger over one of her nipples and lowered his head for a taste of her other breast. As he sucked and caressed, need and want arrowed to her core.

"Oh. *Brady.*" She squeezed and stroked his erection.

He moaned, testing her wetness before sliding in a finger. Then two. "Alicia, I want you so much." His fingers stretched her open. "Not just for this. For everything."

She gazed into his eyes. "Show me," she whispered. "I need you inside me, Officer Jacobs. Now."

His hand skipped down her stomach. "I'll venture south first. With my tongue."

"Later," she murmured, arousal growing at the idea of his future sojourn. "Inside me, Brady. Please." She fished for the packet from the nightstand and tossed the protection at his chest.

He put on the condom, then kissed her deeply. She grasped his shoulders while he lifted his body and parted her legs. He positioned his length at her entrance.

Moaning, she dug her fingernails into his shoulders and thrust her hips.

He slid deep inside her with one quick plunge, filling her with intense pleasure.

She gasped. "*Yes*. Brady, take me there. And I'll take you."

He lifted his head, caressing her cheek as he pumped, kissing her and gazing deeply into her eyes. His hands were on her breasts, her tummy, her rear, between her legs, as they loved each other.

Moving faster. Hearts thumping. Fevered breaths and whispered endearments echoing in her quiet bedroom.

"I'm close," she whispered. "Brady, I'm nearly there."

"I'm right behind you," he whispered in a rough voice. "But as soon as you recuperate, sweetheart, I'm heading south." His voice lowered to an earthy rumble. "And I gotta tell you, baby, I'm *ravenous*."

Alicia panted. She hadn't realized a man's sexy promises could send her over the edge. But in that moment Brady's did. She arched her hips and spun into the stars, grabbing his ass and clinching him close.

He growled with palpable pleasure and lost himself. She shuddered, bucking her hips.

He deepened their kisses, and with dizzying breathlessness she sensed their joined future unfolding before them. She realized with stunning clarity that this sweet, handsome, sexy, patient, and understanding man was the best thing that had ever happened to her.

She and Brady were diving in.

To love and life.

Together.

Don't miss **Just Janie,** the next book in *Love & Other Calamities*!

Just Janie features Janie McAllister, Derek's fraternal twin sister in *Deceiving Derek,* as well as Janie's Canadian cutie, Keon Rivers, a groomsman in the upcoming wedding (if it occurs...)

The story

Just when Janie McAllister is convinced her feelings for her ex are finally and neatly tucked in the past, Keon Rivers surprises everyone—but especially *her*—by coming to town early for a wedding.

OMG, OMG!...okay, she's cool. Janie won't allow the sexy whirlwind that is Keon to toss her world into disorder a second time. No, she'll survive until the nuptials are over and he is on his merry way again.

Except Keon has his own plans. And they involve Janie. And a life together.

That is, if he can get her to see how perfect they truly are together.

Don't miss Just Janie!

Acknowledgments

Any time I have a cop in a story you can bet I've turned to my friend Mary J. Forbes for her expertise and knowledge in all things cop-life-related.

Thank you, Mary, for your knowledge and input and for patiently reading early drafts of *Before Brady* after life "swept in like a rogue wave and whacked me sideways," to paraphrase Alicia Maxwell, the heroine in this book. And thank you for all the idea-bouncing over the years! I am a better writer for it.

Also, I must thank my characters, for refusing to allow me to give up on their stories.

Perseverance is the name of the game.

Turtle on!

Cindy

About the Author

Cindy Procter-King writes steamy romcoms and contemporary romances bursting with laughter and emotion. Sassy feel-good fiction!

Cindy's books are available from eBook retailers all over the world, as well as in trade paperback, some library hard-cover and large print, and some foreign editions.

Cindy lives in Canada with her family, Ghost'Da Allie McBeagle, and too many grand-dogs to count!

For more books and updates, visit:
www.cindyprocter-king.com

facebook.com/cindyprocterkingauthor
instagram.com/cindyprocterking
bookbub.com/authors/cindy-procter-king

Crave another sassy romance?

www.readsassyromance.com

www.ingramcontent.com/pod-product-compliance
Lightning Source LLC
Chambersburg PA
CBHW031053310726
48969CB00007B/2258